I0638884

THE WATCHES
of THE NIGHT

Darcy Lindbergh

Improbable
PRESS

First published by Improbable Press in 2020

Improbable Press is an imprint of:
Clan Destine Press
www.clandestinepress.com.au
PO Box 121, Bittern
Victoria 3918 Australia

National Library of Australia Cataloguing-In-Publication data:

Lindbergh, Darcy

The Watches of the Night

ISBN: 978-0-6488487-4-5 Paperback
ISBN: 978-0-6488487-5-2 E-book

Cover *Gaslight* courtesy of Wikimedia Commons © William Heath Davis House
Cover Design by © Wendy C Fries

Design & Typesetting by Clan Destine Press

Improbable Press
www.improbablepress.co.uk

For fandom, for giving me the courage to tell stories,
for the tables of New Orleans, for helping me decide which story to tell,
and for Leslie, for always believing I could tell this one, and for
every comma in it.

'I left Holmes seated in front of the smouldering fire, and long into the watches of the night I heard the low, melancholy wailings of his violin, and knew that he was still pondering over the strange problem which he had set himself to unravel.'

A Study in Scarlet
Sir Arthur Conan Doyle, 1887

PREFACE

NIGHT FALLS, AND LONDON COMES ALIVE.

Gas lamps sputter into life, gloomy and ineffective against the fog that descends upon the city. There's something wild about London at night, something swift and ruthless that feeds in the shadows, growing and twining insidiously into the brickwork: intrigue and conspiracy, greed and violence, loneliness and fear and despair.

It was into this darkness that Sherlock Holmes cast his light.

I was not surprised to find that Holmes made his detective's living from deeds so often done by cover of night. The night is a natural hiding place, after all, a refuge where no one sees too clearly nor looks too closely, where everyone sins and so no one's sins are counted. Where people shed their masks and become what they truly are, instead of what they pretend to be.

Men are easier to kill in the dark.

And easier, sometimes, to kiss.

So like a magician revealing an impossible trick, Holmes unveiled the depths the night could hold: the secrecy and the mystery, the terror and the beauty, the peril and the peace. He took me, hand in hand, and led me through the shrouded life that's lived between dusk and dawn, and showed me every wondrous, dangerous thing – except for those things which I showed to him.

Night falls.

The adventure begins.

CHAPTER ONE

THE FIRST NIGHT, I LAID AWAKE FOR HOURS.

My injuries often left me awake in the months since I had returned to London, exhausted yet unable to sleep – but this felt different. I had never lain awake out of such keen excitement, with such hope for the morning.

It was the first night after I had met Sherlock Holmes, and *I* felt different.

The offer to share rooms had been unexpected but not unwelcome, and despite Stamford's cautions to me about Holmes' character, I looked forward to meeting him again. He was a curious fellow, with sharp eyes and a quick tongue; his enthusiasm for his experiment had been captivating, and the exchange of our vices both charming and startlingly practical. I found myself quite interested in him, in a way I had been interested in little else since my return to England.

His hands had been bandaged, I remembered; his skin blotched with chemical discolourations. He'd stuck his finger to draw blood – not clumsiness, but carelessness: his physical self subservient to discovery.

I had no idea, that night, what the coming nights might eventually mean to Holmes and I – what we might come to mean to one another. Instead, I remembered his hands, and wondered if my medical expertise may yet be of some use.

I hoped it would be.

It was already well into the evening when Holmes finally arrived at 221B Baker Street with his own possessions. I had spent the day working myself into a state over the prospect of sharing lodgings, being unaccustomed to spending much time in company, and was relieved to finally have my fretting cut short.

I needn't have worried, though. Holmes was genial and accommodating, but after we had spent several hours settling our things, he seemed just as uncertain of himself, just as unused to constant companionship. It set me at ease: we were both unsteady in the society of others, and would therefore have the chance to decide for ourselves how we might best live together.

It was over a late dinner that I broke our tentative silence. 'You knew I had been in Afghanistan, when we met,' I said. 'But I cannot think how you knew to look me up.'

'I didn't,' Holmes chuckled, though he didn't elaborate. 'It's a curious thing – people enjoy hearing things they already know about themselves, when the circumstance is right.' He looked at me from the corner of his eye, as if eager for an invitation, and my interest could not be helped.

'You said yourself we should know each other, if we are to live together,' I said. 'What circumstance could be better?'

Holmes settled himself in front of the fire, settled a pipe between his teeth. For a long moment, he merely looked at me, his eyes sharp and his smile slowly fading into his focus. 'You must tell me if I get anything wrong,' he said, rather sternly.

I readily agreed, but I needn't have bothered – he was right about nearly everything. His declarations ran something like this:

- that I was Scottish by birth, but often spent summers in London; that I had been a lonely child, though he did not comment on my parents;

- that I preferred my tea and liquors strong, and my desserts mild, though before my time abroad it had run the other way around;

- that I had studied at the University of London and at Netley; that I had wanted to be a soldier since I was small;

- that I had been a good student; that I had played rugby somewhat regularly; that I was never in trouble exactly though was not a model of ethics (my breath stopped here, and so did he, without elaborating on the subject);

- that I had landed first in Bombay, before joining the fighting in Candahar; and that I had been shot, but that my actual injury lay more in my mind than in my body.

He continued this way for some time, jumping from my childhood in Edinburgh to my preferences in literature, from my interest in anatomy over chemistry to my inclination toward rereading the papers to calm my nerves. He seemed endlessly amused with each new discovery; I reveled in the details of my life, told back to me.

Yet he insisted this knowledge was only the result of careful observation – the accent in the pronunciation of my consonants, grown lazy with comfort as the night wore on – the significances of the curiosities I had picked up in the subcontinent – a certain text on my shelf – a certain stain on my fingers.

It was not, as one might have supposed, anything like being picked apart: it was like being identified. Not picked apart, but picked out: noticed, for the first time since I had disappeared with my ruined health and devastated career into the drain of London.

It was a test, I realised, of my limitations, a scouting of my boundaries; I found, to his obvious delight, that I had very few.

'You have a keen eye,' I exclaimed. 'Quite incredible.'

'A blessing and a curse both,' he answered modestly, but I could tell he was pleased as he settled back into his chair, having apparently exhausted himself: he could not hide his blush.

The dreams began something like this: the air was heavy and cloying, thick with the smell of bodies and gunpowder. Overhead, the dark Afghani night was a velvet blue, pricked with the diamond white of stars and shrouded in smoke.

The sky was the only thing fantastic or exotic about Afghanistan. There was no magic in that land; there was only the rank and rot of death and fear, the deceptive sweetness of starvation, the sour stench of infection.

Then the dreams shifted, and a voice cried out – not in pain, this time. 'Watson! Come and have a drink with us.'

I looked over: the boys by the fire looked back, exhausted and dirty but whole, complete men, eyes and limbs still in their places, wounds smoothed over by their tired smiles. A bottle passed between them, but I knew it wasn't really whisky they were offering. I sighed and smiled back and heaved myself up to rejoin them.

When I woke, I lay in bed for hours, wondering whether it had been a dream or a nightmare, a blessing or a curse: sitting under that sky with men who never made it home, sharing a drink and a memory that never happened, laughing as though there was still breath in their lungs.

As though I had never left them behind.

Though I had not been on a battlefield in months, I was still not used to silent nights; my thoughts were too free to dwell on things better forgotten. My future, confined by my injuries, suddenly unfolded prophetically before me: a ceaseless parade of quiet and calm, leaving me forever trapped in the memory of war, waiting for a call to arms that was never going to come.

Finally I attempted an escape to the sitting room, but it wasn't empty. Holmes looked up from his chair by the fire, surprised; I drew back, apologetic. 'I didn't mean to disturb you.'

'Not at all,' Holmes said, recovering himself. 'Please, come and sit. I don't mind the company, and you look like you would be better for it.'

I hesitated, but he beckoned me forward and even lit my pipe for me before falling back into his thoughtful silence.

There was an intensely private air about Holmes sometimes, I thought, but there was something else, too, something that seemed to reach out. Perhaps it was not such a coincidence after all, to have found him alone and expectant by the fire. He did not say another word to me that night, nor I to him, but we were there together all the same, and suddenly the silence was much easier to bear.

CHAPTER TWO

IN THE FIRST WEEKS OF SHARING ROOMS WITH HOLMES, I FREQUENTLY thought that if only I were privy to the conversations he held with his perplexing array of clients, I might better understand his business, and thus more of Holmes himself. Even his title – a consulting detective – failed to satisfy my curiosity, so when at last he invited me to join him for a case, I was thrilled that I might finally uncover his mysteries.

How wrong I was!

Oh, I did better understand his work; indeed, once he laid out his reasoning, it seemed astonishing that I had been so blind. But the enigma of Holmes himself only deepened – how had he learned such skills? How had he the abilities to walk with police as comfortably as ruffian children? How did he so easily lay traps for murderers and wrestle them into submission?

Holmes listened intently as Jefferson Hope recounted his tale, but I could scarcely pay attention to it; I confess I was, instead, entranced by Holmes himself, wondering what conclusions he was drawing from each word, wondering whether he had some secret to know if they were the truth. If he could look into the darkness and tease out the light.

My nerves, I suddenly realised, were calm; when Holmes looked back at me, his eyes were bright.

The most irritating thing about Sherlock Holmes' vanity, I thought afterward, when the papers began publishing their accounts of the Jefferson Hope murders, was how very deserved it was. Watching

Holmes in action on the case, I had been surprised and impressed; now, having understood his meticulous analysis of the facts, I knew he deserved more credit than he had got. 'Credit doesn't concern me,' he told me one night, flinging another paper that had made no mention of him down into a stack. 'It's only the work that matters.'

It might have been convincing, but for the scorn in his voice.

He also said, when I threatened to put down an accurate account of the case, that I ought to do as I liked. I hadn't taken it seriously at first, but watching him now, it struck me that perhaps I ought to take him at his word. My notes on the matter were not entirely complete, but I was sure if I thought carefully, I could remember enough about the case to write an account out well enough to be published, and I might even make an admirable job of it.

And concerned with credit or not, I knew from experience that Holmes could be flattered; surely, I thought, a little acclaim would ease away some of that bitterness.

'How do you decide which volume they go into?' I asked a few evenings later, picking up one of the scraps Holmes was pasting into his complicated filing system. My curiosity in his methods was piqued, and I wanted to know more. '*Vampirism in Hungary* – under V? or H?'

'It depends upon which part one is more likely to require,' Holmes instructed easily, his pride in his index evident. 'As a singular topic, *Hungary* is too broad to be of any real use. *Vampirism*, on the other hand – ' He looked up, questioning. 'Isn't that only a myth, a superstition?'

'Yet men are superstitious. I suppose I would file it under V.'

Holmes was visibly delighted. 'Precisely! That's precisely it. And so it goes, always with an eye toward the detecting business. Then you'll always be able to find what you're looking for.'

'And if what you're looking for isn't here?'

'Then you look elsewhere, Watson. Everything is discoverable. One must only not give up too early.'

'I shall try not to,' I promised.

Holmes studied me a moment. Quietly, almost shyly, he added, 'Then I shall be very glad to trust you.'

I thought of my fledgling attempt to write an account of his work, hidden away in my room, and hoped he meant with more than just his books.

'Watson?'

Holmes' voice was soft in the dark, tinged with concern. I squeezed my eyes shut, hoping he would think me asleep and go away, but instead he crept closer toward my bed. 'Watson, are you all right?'

I sighed, caught out; the summer had grown long and hot, and I was not faring well in it. 'Just a headache. Some nausea. It will pass.'

'The enteric fever,' Holmes deduced. 'It still flares up sometimes.'

'It's not unusual.'

'No,' he agreed. 'Is there anything I can do for you?'

I looked up; in the moonlight, Holmes' eyes were pale with worry. 'No,' I managed, though he seemed in earnest. 'I can only wait for it to pass.'

He shifted on his feet. 'I could bring you a cup of tea.'

'Mrs Hudson will have gone to bed already.'

'I'm sure I can manage,' he insisted, indignant at the implication that he could not, and went to prove himself.

He did, in fact, come back some time later – and if it was much later than it would have taken Mrs Hudson, I chose not to mention it. He set a cup on the bedside table and pressed a cool cloth to my forehead. 'Thank you,' I said.

'You're quite welcome,' Holmes said softly. 'I hope that by tomorrow you are feeling better.'

My tomorrow was not, in fact, any better.

'Oh, for God's sake – ' I slammed my book shut in disgust as I looked up at the clock again. It was half past eleven in the evening: only three minutes later than it had been since the last time I had checked.

There was still no sign of Holmes.

He'd set off hours ago, disguised as a dock worker and intending to situate himself in a few disreputable pubs to listen to the gossip, hoping for some word of the whereabouts of some notoriously dangerous criminal. Although by now quite familiar with his work, tonight I worried: he would be in danger if he were caught, and there was no one to aid him. Once again, I cursed my health – would that I could've been a trustworthy fellow to have at his back.

Finally I heard the turn of the latch-key in the door, and was on my feet in an instant.

'Watson,' Holmes exclaimed when he saw me, clapping his hands together. 'Good, you're awake. I must tell you everything.'

He was fine, of course. 'I'm ready to hear it,' I managed, trying to hide my relief from Holmes' attention. I could not tamp it down entirely, though – for the first time all night, I felt as though I could breathe.

CHAPTER THREE

IN THOSE FIRST MONTHS AT BAKER STREET I HEALED, THOUGH NOT entirely. The fevers became less frequent; the ache of my shoulder and thigh less troublesome. Holmes began bullying me out of the flat on occasion, slowing his long gait so I could walk beside him through Regent's Park, deducing passersby, or else taking me to dinner in the Domino Room or down Fleet Street whenever the irregularity of my appetite was brought to his attention. In return, I began bullying him about his use of narcotics, fussing about the negative effects on his mind and his person whenever I had the chance.

We were neither of us terribly at ease with society at large – Holmes being somewhat of a Bohemian in character, and myself being somewhat averse to strangers or crowds – but as 1881 passed inevitably into 1882, and then 1882 to 1883, so too did we pass inevitably from simply sharing rooms into an easy friendship.

'Did you know,' he said some January night, blowing blue smoke into the room, 'We've been sharing rooms two years now, Watson.'

'Have we? It hardly seems so long.'

'And yet it seems as if we've always done, doesn't it?'

There was a smile curving around his pipe. 'It does,' I agreed, surprising myself. 'How easily time does seem to pass us by.'

'Strange,' I said to Holmes, as we waited together in the dark for Helen Stoner's signal, 'Until now I don't believe I've been out of London since I came back from India.'

'Stoke Moran is hardly a resort town. Perhaps next time we shall take a case by the sea, Watson. What do you say?'

'I say wherever it is you have a case, I am your man.'

His eyes glinted in the dark; his voice was thick with satisfaction. 'I didn't realise you had such interest in the detective business.'

'I daresay it breaks up the monotony of life.'

'Do you think we lead a monotonous life?'

'I certainly don't think you do.'

'Is your own life too monotonous?'

'It could do with a little shake-up now and then.'

'Once you told me your nerves could not withstand a row. Can they now withstand the difficulty of a case like this? The tension? The waiting? The dangerous crossing of the land at night?'

'I daresay it would do them some good, in fact, and sometimes we row anyway.'

He laughed brightly, his long fingers pressing lightly upon my wrist. 'Good,' he said firmly. 'Now look – there's our signal. Let's see if we can put an end to Dr. Roylott's terror, and finally solve the mystery of this supposed speckled band.'

Following the Roylott case, Holmes did hold true to his word, and I did find myself now involved in a series of fascinating little problems. Of course most of Holmes' cases he solved from the comfort of our sitting-room, and I either listened in or kept to myself, depending on how interesting they were.

Sometimes, however, a simple case became something much more dire, and led to Holmes banging up the stairs to my room sometime past midnight. 'So sorry to disturb you,' he said breathlessly, slumping into my chair as I hurried from my bed into a dressing gown. 'But there are certain conveniences to having a doctor in the house, and I'm afraid I must call upon them.' And he took his hand from his forehead, revealing a bloody gash.

'Holmes!' I cried, and immediately set to work. The blood had pooled along his hairline, and once the gash was clean, I set two stitches in, cursing at the poor light. 'It will serve you right if it scars,' I told him. 'You must be more careful, Holmes.'

'I promise,' he said soberly, his fingers catching on my wrist. He did not cry out, but I could see the pain in his eyes, and I gentled my touch as well as I could, into barely more than a brush.

As I was creeping up the stairs a week later, I hoped Holmes would have already gone to bed, that I might be able to slink into our rooms with him none the wiser, to lick my wounds in peace.

But Lady Luck had already proved she was not on my side tonight, and Holmes was still sprawled out on the sofa where I had left him earlier. What was worse: he'd been joined by a syringe, which was on the floor beside him.

'You can't say you wish I wouldn't,' he said softly, barely opening his eyes to study me, 'when you yourself have been out engaging in your vices.'

'There's not so much danger at the tables as there is in that bottle,' I said, but I knew he was right. There was nothing wrong with a card game or the occasional bet, but some weakness in me made it difficult to walk away even when my chances of winning were next to none.

I had resisted the tables for years, with my occasional locum work and Holmes' cases to distract me. It seemed the distraction was no longer strong enough.

'You are the pot,' he sighed, his head falling back. 'And I am the kettle. We have both been in the fire, Watson, and we are both black.'

Other nights, we laughed.

'Hush!' Holmes scolded, pulling me up several steps into a doorway halfway down some foul alley. I struggled against the laughter in my chest, but Holmes' plea for silence would have been easier to manage had he himself not been shaking with mirth.

I didn't try very hard; I needed the laughter.

Footsteps echoed throughout the alley behind us. Our pursuer snarled and growled, but the sound was too high and thin to be threatening, and I had to bury my face into my arm so that my giggle would not be heard.

Finally the footsteps retreated, and I could safely look up, but one glance at Holmes' face again and I fell back into laughter. 'I'm sorry,' I said, trying to catch my breath. 'I hardly know what came over me.'

Holmes clapped his hand to my shoulder. 'I'm afraid the problem was,' he said as somberly as possible, 'that the gentleman was ridiculous,' and we burst into laughter again.

Once we collected ourselves, Holmes leapt from our hiding place and turned to offer me his hand, helping me down. His fingers were warm and strong beneath mine; when he let go, I clenched my hand in my coat to ease the feeling of their heat on my skin before the memory could settle into my bones.

CHAPTER FOUR

A FIST FLEW AND THE CROWD CHEERED IN UNISON, AN UGLY, FEROCIOUS jeer that swelled and swooped as the fight went on. Holmes was a blur in the centre, his usually pristine brow flushed and sweaty, his cheeks and chin smudged with dirt, his grin stretched wide and taunting. I could see the joy in his face too, the power and the freedom and the adrenalin pumping through his veins. Through his heart.

My own beat faster.

Holmes wasn't the strongest in the circle, but he was likely the fastest and certainly the cleverest. He took on his opponents fiercely, dodging their blows and using their weight and their predictability against them for victory after victory.

But even Sherlock Holmes was not infallible, and by the time he slipped out of the circle and back toward me, he was bleeding from a cut above his eye and scrapes bloomed across his cheeks. His weight settled unevenly on his hips too, as though favouring a bruised rib or two.

'I think that's it for tonight,' I said, letting Holmes lean heavily on my shoulder, leading him away.

'As you say, Doctor,' Holmes allowed, laughing and gasping. He submitted to my prodding fingers, and when I was satisfied, I submitted in turn to watching the remaining matches as he studied the other boxers.

We were nearly home when we first heard the sound: a high-pitched whimper. A plea of pain.

Holmes stopped mid-sentence, cutting off our comparison of

the night's boxers to the eventual champion to listen carefully. The sound came again, louder, and he was off in a flash, darting down an alley in search of its source.

He found it tucked behind a jumble of abandoned crates: a grey-brown dog with matted fur and a leg crusted with blood. 'Here, doggy,' he cooed, digging through his pockets for something to entice the creature with and finding half a biscuit. 'Here, boy.'

The dog shrank back in fear, but Holmes waited patiently, murmuring gentle encouragements, until at last the animal shuffled forward and quickly took the biscuit from his fingers. I watched with not a little awe – I'd never seen Holmes so tender – and finally made my way forward to examine the bloody leg. 'Broken, I think.'

'Miserable thing,' Holmes agreed. After a few long minutes of quiet petting and cooing, Holmes was able to gather the dog into his arms, heedless of his coat. 'I know a fellow who will be able to fix this up in no time,' he said, hoisting the dog up, trying not to jostle him. 'He'll be able to find a proper home for the poor boy.'

I admit that I drifted for several years. My constitution, though healed, would never be the same as it had been before the war, and I was an old man already at the age of thirty. Perhaps I should have set up a practice, for my banking-account was never flush, but I satisfied my obligations and myself with odd here-and-there positions whenever the need arose.

At any rate, my eccentric companion never said a word of my idleness.

I actually thought Holmes enjoyed having me about the rooms. He was a solitary sort naturally, though good-natured; he was also peculiarly exacting in his habits, and preferred to have them unchanged. I supposed I had simply become a part of those habits – an audience for his ejaculations, a ready assistant in his myriad experiments. I occasionally sat in on his cases, though I just as often disappeared up to my own bedroom instead; more often, I accompanied him to the music halls, or to dinner, or even once or twice to the laboratories at St Bart's Hospital.

I was comfortable. More than that, I was content. Holmes kept me on my feet as often as he left me to my own devices, and as we quietly marked the passing of each January, there was nowhere else I would have preferred to be.

It was nearing midnight, one warm September night in 1887, when there was a furious pounding on the door downstairs. Holmes and I had stayed up late, sharing a brandy and discussing some new philosophical theory of the self – 'Rot,' Holmes had said, and I'd rejoined, 'Rot, but,' not quite agreeing – and so he went to investigate before Mrs Hudson could be drawn out. He returned some minutes later accompanied by a shaking man, struck pale with fright.

'My friend and colleague, Doctor Watson,' Holmes introduced. 'Watson, Mr Terrence Hesse.'

'My apologies for the hour, sir,' Hesse said, terribly politely. 'It's only that I'm afraid for my life.'

'Let me pour you a brandy for the nerves,' Holmes said, his voice low and soothing. 'You are quite safe here. Now tell us your story.'

Hesse told an extraordinary tale about a job he'd taken laying tile in the hall of a large Kensington home, being paid far too much, and how the master of the house had been violently killed. Hesse, working just outside the gentleman's study, had heard nothing at all, but the entire household staff had accused him of the crime.

'They pointed at me!' he cried. 'Though each should have known I was in the hall all the while, by the noise I was making. Even the butler!'

'And you ran?' Holmes surmised.

'What else was there to do? My wages don't care for just my own upkeep, sir. I share rooms with another fellow, a tile-layer like myself, though he's been out of work from an accident these past weeks. I went out the back as quick as I could and rushed home to him, but I could hardly stay where they'd have found me. I'd heard your name, sir, from the street Arabs, and thought I'd see if you could help me.'

A lesser man might have thought that Hesse's story was an

obvious lie intended to save himself, but Holmes' caution in meting out justice was firm, and he was staunch in his refusal to jump to conclusions.

'And you say you heard nothing from the study?' Holmes asked, putting his fingers to his lips in thought.

'None, sir.'

'And each of the household staff accused you, to a man?'

'All of them, sir, even those I had not seen. But tile-laying – it's fine work, you know, but there's a fair amount of tapping and other noise that goes on. They must have heard me at it.'

Holmes hummed, muttering to himself for a moment, then went for his hat and coat. 'Come, Watson,' he directed. 'We must get to the bottom of this grotesque business.'

The Hesse case had led Holmes and I on a chase through the slick dark streets of London, ending with swift fists and Holmes' triumphant cry rising into the night. He'd been panting with excitement, disheveled and bruising beautifully around the eye, and I'd been drawn in, transfixed by his energy.

By the time I fell into bed, the adrenalin in my veins had transformed into something hot and golden in my spine, in my belly, my groin. It bloomed insistently, where there had been nothing for years – not since the Jezail bullet. Not since the fever.

There was definitely something there now: something novel and unexpected and so very *missed*.

I struggled against my nightshirt and closed a hand around my prick, somehow surprised to find myself hard even though I felt the demand, the eagerness. I wanted to take my time, to *enjoy* it, but as soon as I touched myself, urgency slid into desperation. My hand rushed along my shaft, twisted at the head in an old familiar fashion; my pace quickened, rising to the edge; I thought about running, and about fighting, and about the crook of Holmes' smile, the shine of his eyes, his face as he turned to me, breathless and victorious – and I came, I came *hard*, and my mind went completely, blissfully blank.

Simpson's was busy on the next evening, the late-night wanderers drawn toward the promise of a hot cup of coffee or a sandwich. Across the table, Holmes seemed to revel in the noise, his eyes glowing and his hands fluttering as he recounted some story of his youth.

I was barely listening to him. Instead I was watching, following Holmes' fingers as they moved from his coffee spoon to his mouth, to settle on his leg before wandering off again. His cheeks were flushed, first from the excitement of the case – a tawdry little bit of counterfeiting, but a thrilling arrest nonetheless – and now from the coffee and the heat of the room, and I wondered how warm those cheeks would be to the touch. Would he turn his head into my hand, if I reached out?

The thought took me off-guard and I sat back, suddenly realising how far I'd leaned forward. It had been a long time since I had had a thought like that, and I knew it was not one of a devoted friend. It was a thought of gentleness, of intimacy. It spoke of an affection that ran too deep in places that ought to have been reserved, set aside for someone else.

Of – attraction.

When I sipped at my coffee again, it had gone bitter.

Fog rolled in.

London drifted through the hazy sea for days, damp seeping drearily into the corners of Baker Street, settling an uneasy silence over everything like a thin coating of dust. My leg and shoulder ached constantly, but no matter how high the fire was built, I could not shake the chill.

The sober atmosphere seemed to set Holmes on edge as well, and he was in and out of our rooms at all hours of the day and night with barely a word to me. His long absences left me feeling as alone as I had been before moving into 221B, and I could not help but wonder whether he had been driven out into the night by something he had seen in *me* – something I was only barely starting to see in myself.

It would not have been the first time Holmes had known

something about me before I knew it myself, after all. He knew so much at a single glance – there was no telling what sharing rooms with someone might reveal to him.

Outside, the fog curled thick and yellow against the windowpanes, and finally I took myself to bed to escape from it. I would find no resolutions that night anyway, no answers: the darkness was too impenetrable, and the future, I feared, too bleak.

CHAPTER FIVE

I WAS GOING TO CALL IT *A STUDY IN SCARLET*, I HAD DECIDED, BUT now as I flipped through the pages, I wondered whether it was fit for publication after all, even with an offer to print already on my desk. Each of my exclamations of awe and admiration now seemed illicit, written proofs of a prurient curiosity. As filthy and felonious as the murderer Holmes had brought to heel.

But it hadn't been like that, I knew. Whatever new thing had sprung into my chest, it was a young, weak thing, and it had nothing to do with the impression Holmes had made upon me when first we met, nor anything to do with the healing I had undergone at 221B Baker Street, nor with the decision to write our adventure down. Was I now to let this callow thing paint my memories with so red a brush?

No.

There was no danger, I told myself, because *A Study in Scarlet* was not about me in any way. It was about Holmes, and Holmes deserved it: the credit, the understanding. I would not allow my cowardice to take that from him now.

I would accept this offer to publish; I was determined. I put aside my fears and, swallowing hard, instead picked up the letter from the publisher at *Beeton's*.

Yet, haunted by my own mind, I could not sleep. Every muted clink of glass from the sitting room resonated along my nerves; every hint of Holmes' presence beyond my bedroom door left me straining to glean something from the clues and impressions his quiet movements gave me.

I could imagine him, still sitting exactly where I'd left him hours before, still tense and silent at his microscope. His hands would be careful, his long fingers graceful and gentle with his delicate instruments. His great working mind would be a palpable energy in the room, vibrating with white-hot intensity as he built and connected and deduced and *understood*.

My imagination slipped away from me then, into an onslaught of images that left me choking for air: my hand on his shoulder, warm; his eyes lighting with recognition, with *response*. Those extravagant fingers, entwining with mine, pulling me closer. Arousal slid heavily into my veins.

And then: the soft strains of a violin melted through the door. Holmes had heard my breath stop, I realised, had been keeping part of himself wary for sounds of distress. Had mistaken my gasp of arousal for one of fear, of a nightmare. Had abandoned his work to soothe me.

I lay awake, listening to the sound as though it were a penance. My eyes burned.

Holmes' breath blew a visible plume into the night air. 'Soon,' he promised, unprompted, and I did my best not to grumble. The rooftop we had made our seat was not a comfortable lookout, exposed as it was to the wind; I was exhausted from a lack of sleep the night before and longed for the warmth of Baker Street.

'If it *isn't* soon,' I returned, 'you'll be taking home a frozen statue instead of a man.'

Holmes did not answer, but his lips twitched – a smile he wasn't ready to give in to but couldn't help. I reminded myself forcefully that whatever I felt to see that smile, it was a feeling I alone experienced. That Holmes had noticed my discomfort was only indicative of his nature as a detective. He was a friend to me, a good one – and I was not a very good one in return.

Perhaps I had simply grown too used to Holmes' company, I thought; perhaps I had grown too unused to the company of women. Perhaps I ought to apply myself to finding a wife, to building a separate home and a separate life.

Yes, I resolved. A wife.

I was leaning into Holmes, I realised, seeking protection from the cold. I flushed, embarrassed, and shifted away, sliding further down our makeshift bench.

The terrible business of Pondicherry Lodge was, at once, the best and the worst case I could have imagined.

It was clear that Holmes could not do without a case a moment longer. He had been indulging in his cocaine for weeks, and no argument could be had to stop him; he had turned melancholy and despondent. Looking back on that period, years later, I would wonder whether it was my own despair that prompted his, but at the time, I foolishly thought Holmes too wrapped up in his drugs and dramatics to notice my troubles.

But then there was Miss Mary Morstan.

Miss Morstan was a fair, wide-eyed creature, with the sort of grace only bad luck can grant a person, yet still with an inordinate amount of hope. Whether I was merely drawn to her out of the juxtaposition to Holmes, or whether because she herself was drawn to me, I could not say. The facts remained: we were drawn to one another, and though the case turned out to be a dark and wicked affair, I would not soon forget standing in the gardens of Pondicherry Lodge, holding her hand, turning toward each other for protection and comfort.

Her hand was a soft, warm thing – so very unlike Holmes', which were, I recalled, always so scarred and battered.

'Miss Mary Morstan,' Holmes drawled, interrupting our comfortable silence with a disdainful tone. 'A singular woman, to have caught your eye.'

I looked up from my papers. I wanted to defend myself against the implication that I had been in some way ensnared, but in truth I had been, these last weeks, so I flushed instead of denying it. Miss

29

Morstan had been charming, kind, gentle: everything any reasonable man hoped a wife might be.

The subject of which was fast becoming something of a pressing interest. I felt it was only a matter of time before Holmes determined that there had been a change in the nature of my devotion to him, if he hadn't already. The appearance of Mary Morstan as soon as I had decided to start looking earnestly for a wife seemed like an act of providence, and I thought – I hoped – that I could love her. I at least intended to try my hand at it.

'You liked her as well,' I said, in a poor attempt at deflection.

'I did,' he agreed. 'She was an ideal client. But I suspect you intend to make more of her than that.'

'I intend nothing,' I lied, but I immediately felt guilty for it. I tried to shrug it away. 'It's hard to say what fate will bring.'

As my association with Miss Morstan began growing deeper, so did my association with Holmes begin to grow fragile.

At first I put this down as a natural consequence of spending many of my evenings elsewhere, but I soon came to realise that even when I was at home, Holmes seemed withdrawn, unlikely to ask for assistance or an opinion. The invitations to this or that lecture or opera dwindled rapidly, and he was as like as not to be out until long after I had already gone to bed.

Good, I told myself. *If this does end the way I hope, we will have to get used to spending time apart.*

I did not get used to it.

As pleasurable as I found Mary's company, it wasn't a substitute for the companionship of such a friend. I found myself opening more and more conversations, which Holmes responded to haltingly; I found myself making excuses to Mary, simply to end up at home, dithering over my dinner and waiting for Holmes to come back.

Finally, about three months after Mary's case had been resolved, I found an opportunity. 'I say, Holmes,' I said one afternoon while we puttered around the flat together. 'My muscles have gone quite tight. What do you say we go and spend an evening at the bathhouse?'

To my surprise, he agreed, and we were off together. He had a fondness for the Turkish bath; he was fastidious about his hygiene, of course, and I had often said before that, as a method of relaxation, the baths were far more conducive to his health than was his cocaine.

We were quiet as we made our way and eventually found ourselves a pair of sofas in a secluded corner of the drying-room. We settled back, draped in our towels, and drifted.

'You've been busy lately,' I remarked eventually. 'Anything good?'

'No busier than you,' Holmes hummed, but there was no bite in it. 'I've had a client, actually, with an interesting problem regarding an inheritance.'

'You solved it, I presume?'

He had, and there was a little smile around his mouth as he recounted the facts to me, and for a while I could forget that there was anything amiss between us – that I had ever thought anything unsuitable toward my friend; that I had dinner reservations the next evening with Miss Morstan; that I had begun making the plans for a small, intimate wedding, a new home for a new couple, a livelihood in a medical practice.

I could forget that I had begun to plan a life separated from him, as it eventually had to be.

CHAPTER SIX

THE BODY LEFT ON CARLTON RODGERS' DINING ROOM FLOOR HAD been reduced, through some villain's rage and fury, to no more than shreds. I did what examination I could as quickly as possible and immediately turned away from it, trying to overwrite the sudden memory of Afghanistan washing through my mind with the thought of where I was supposed to have been that evening: at dinner with Miss Morstan, where there might have been wine and flirtations at the table instead of a body under it.

'Watson – *Watson*. Pay attention. Is there or isn't there blood on that rug?'

I started, Holmes' voice dragging me back to the murderous present, and looked down to see a few pale red drops strewn across the carpets. 'Ah, yes. Yes, there is. My apologies, Holmes, I was distracted.'

Holmes huffed, exasperated. 'This is intolerable,' he said. 'If you cannot focus, you should have gone with Miss Morstan and saved me the trouble.'

I stared, taken aback. 'Holmes,' I began, but he waved his hand.

'I won't need you here, Watson. You might as well go and salvage your dinner plans.'

My stomach curdled with embarrassment: I had been dismissed. I watched as he promptly forgot me, ignoring me as he laid out on the floor with his magnifying glass, examining the drops of blood.

I waited hours for an opportune moment, but it was no good. Holmes hadn't looked up from his experiment even once since I arrived home; I had to interrupt him.

'Holmes,' I began. 'I must tell you something.'

'No,' he cut in, his tone surprisingly cold and distant. 'I already know what you're going to say, and I don't particularly need to hear it. I cannot congratulate you anyway. It's perfectly fearful.'

I gaped. I had not expected Holmes to rejoice, it's true, but neither had I expected him to begrudge me the news. 'It's perfectly expected,' I said. 'Falling in love, getting married. You must have known I would someday.'

Holmes grimaced. 'Of course not. You have never done what was expected of you, Watson.'

'It's *natural*,' I argued, now a little offended.

'It's *weakness*,' he threw back, and I recoiled from the sudden severity of his features. 'It clouds the judgement. One cannot see clearly where one allows oneself to become biased.'

The ache I felt at the prospect of leaving Baker Street sharpened under his derision, and I reminded myself sternly that this was precisely why I had to go, why I had to marry: I could no longer see Holmes clearly, and my heart would break if I did not first ruin myself with all my *bias*.

Married life suited me, as I expected. The joy of sharing a home with a wife – with whom I could be at ease, with whom I did not have to hide my desires – was unparalleled, and I was as satisfied as could be. Mary was free with her affection and laughter, kind and quiet in the evening hours, efficient and productive in her days. She read, played music, kissed as sweetly as an apricot in spring, gasped my name in awe and astonishment – there was nothing lacking in her.

And if I occasionally sat by the fire and let my thoughts drift to Sherlock Holmes, to the rooms I'd left behind and the adventures I'd had to put away these last months, it was only the nostalgia of an aging man embarking on the next era of his life.

Holmes had not been there, the day I left. He'd gone to investigate a problem of his brother's the evening before, and, I assumed, stayed overnight in Pall Mall. I reminded myself of that often, actually, whenever I questioned myself as to why I'd left Baker Street. I'd waited, that last night; I'd stayed up, hoping to share one last glass of brandy, one last pipe, watching the hours slowly tick away.

I'd waited all night, but he had not come back.

Though my marriage and my practice kept me busy, I quickly picked up writing as a habit as well. Soon I was writing more consistently than I had ever written at Baker Street; productivity suited me, and I found that the quiet evening hours were quite suited to putting down a narrative now that there were no experimentations or exclamations to distract me.

It was only natural to put down the case that had brought Mary and I together. I gathered up my notes and put pen to paper, occasionally going to find her and ask her about this or that detail, whether she remembered what was said, or what she recalled of Thaddeus Sholto's exotic parlour. The exercise brought us closer together, I felt; she delighted in being the subject of such a story. Holmes, in the same position, had only ever scoffed and sneered. He could not endure the romance of it; Mary, for obvious reasons, could.

There were a few letters between Holmes and I, of course, but the distance between us grew, as new marriages are wont to do to old friendships. It was with a pang of remorse that I realised I now spent more time with my fictional Holmes than with the original; I resolved soon to visit the original counterpart of flesh and bone.

It was weeks before I allowed myself, however, and now, with not a little guilt, the familiar black door of 221B Baker Street rose out of the misty evening before me like a beacon. I had tried, with all the strength of necessity and good judgement, not to even dream of it, but I missed Holmes terribly and convinced myself a single visit from one friend to another would do no harm.

But Mrs Hudson did not smile when she answered the door. 'Oh, dear me,' she said instead. 'Only – he's not in, Doctor Watson. He'll be sorry to have missed you, but he told me not to expect him until late.'

'Oh,' I said, overcome with awkwardness. Somehow it hadn't occurred to me that he might not be there, and suddenly I felt like a fool. Had I expected him to wait for me, to hold himself in stasis until I returned? Of course not. I stepped back toward the door. 'I should have – do tell him I called.'

Mrs Hudson promised she would, and I rushed away, losing myself in the thinning foot-traffic of the evening. I was not expected home for hours yet. I was not expected anywhere at all, actually, and I wandered London until I hardly knew where I was, or where I ought to be.

The wire that arrived just after the next day's suppertime said, without preamble: *Your assistance and medical bag required. - S.H.* The number for Inspector Lestrade's office at Scotland Yard followed.

Worry warred with delight. I was thrilled to be called upon again, and yet the requirement of my medical bag spoke to my darkest fears – that Sherlock Holmes had gone into dire danger without me, and paid the price for my absence with injury and pain. My imagination ran wild with terrible possibilities, and I rushed to Lestrade's office, bursting through the door – only to find Holmes, upright and tidy, nursing a cigarette, and the Inspector himself, scowling and filthy, nursing a swollen purple finger.

'If you'll attend to Lestrade,' Holmes said, smiling in lieu of a hello, 'I should like your opinion on our case, Watson.'

Relief washed through me. 'You're not hurt?'

Holmes' smile turned soft, almost fondly apologetic. 'Not I, it's Lestrade that's had the unfortunate run in with a murderer. Now we are tasked with finding the culprit. Are you in?'

Some small, traitorous part of me was actually disappointed it was not Holmes who required my medical attention. I stomped it down, horrified. 'I am your man,' I said, and as Holmes began explaining the case, I knelt next to Lestrade and opened my bag.

'You could stay, if you liked,' Holmes said after the case concluded. 'Whenever Mrs Watson is away.'

He was, by all appearances, intent on his chemical tests, but his back was unnaturally straight, his hands slow and deliberate: he was uncertain.

'Stay here?' I repeated, surprised. My pleasure at the unexpected invitation must have been obvious, though; I had made it more than clear that I had missed Baker Street in the months since my marriage. 'You wouldn't mind?'

Holmes shrugged, carefully nonchalant, though I could hear a smile curling around his voice. 'There's no reason for you to be alone when there is a room here. Especially as it's still fitted out with a comfortable bed, and the flat with a familiar companion.'

'Convenient,' I said, trying not to laugh.

'I thought so,' he smirked, but a moment later he said, more seriously, 'Mrs Hudson would be pleased to have you home, I think. Despite her tenant's occasional clients, she does lead a surprisingly solitary life.'

At this, my smile faded. 'Mrs Hudson is always welcome to dinner with Mrs Watson and I,' I said gently, not wanting to break the spell of his concealed confession.

Holmes' back straightened further. 'Perhaps,' he said vaguely. 'Still. The upstairs room is always available, Watson. A weekend visit would never be a burden.'

I soon took the invitation to heart, arriving at Baker Street, outfitted to stay for the weekend as Mary went to visit her friend Mrs Cecil Forrester. I was pleasantly surprised to find a fire in the hearth and Holmes still awake on the sofa. 'Hullo,' I called, taking off my coat. 'Is there a case on?'

'Oh,' Holmes said, after a too-long pause. 'Watson, it's you.'

A chill washed over me upon hearing his voice, thick as it was. 'Holmes, are you all right?'

'Oh, yes,' he answered, and giggled unexpectedly. 'I am seven-percent of all right.'

My heart sank. When I rounded the sofa, the evidence abandoned on the floor was unmistakable: the glass bottle, the accompanying syringe. Deceptively medicinal. Terribly neat.

'Oh, Holmes.' I gathered the accoutrements up. 'Cocaine, was it?'

'Just the usual dosage,' Holmes agreed.

'I wish you wouldn't.' I put one hand to his forehead and took his pulse with the other – he was warm, his pulse quick, but neither dangerously so. My hands lingered anyway, pushing back his hair, counting his heartbeats.

Holmes' mouth was a horrible, twisted line. 'I know you do,' he said quietly, but he made no promises. We both knew he would not be able to keep them if he did.

'Come on,' I said. 'Let's get you to bed.'

CHAPTER SEVEN

'HE'S NOT WELL,' I CONFIDED IN MARY WHEN I RETURNED HOME THE following weekend. 'I shall have to go round more often, if you aren't too bothered by it.'

'Not at all,' Mary said, with a sympathetic smile. Not for the first time, I counted myself very lucky to have as a wife someone that had known Holmes as a mercurial detective before knowing him as my friend. 'You do think he'll be all right?'

'It's gotten worse,' I admitted, 'swinging back and forth wildly between activity and apathy, taking cases without rest and then drugging himself into oblivion. But he's made it through these periods before. I've no cause to think he won't again.'

But I was worried. He refused outright to be roused, and I somehow felt that I had lost my right to manhandle him around the flat, to force him to the breakfast table or out for a brief walk. It was a strange, helpless feeling, being closer to him than I'd been in months and yet too far away to make a difference.

'Then he will,' Mary said, 'if only because you believe it of him.'

I kissed her then, and let myself be comforted, but I knew the truth: if it even could be his cure, it would have to be a mighty strong belief.

What relief there was for me, when next I saw Holmes! – he was not only tidy and upright, but energetic, with a gleam in his eye. Once again he turned that eye upon me, so reminiscent of our first night at Baker Street, deducing an incorrigible servant girl as well as a walk through the wet country, and I laughed in pleasure, no longer afraid of his deductions.

There was a case on, which I had suspected, and I had no sooner inspected the letter that had begun it, than we were receiving the King of Bohemia himself.

'I hadn't realised that you were in the habit of receiving royalty,' I remarked, as soon as he'd gone.

Holmes laughed. 'I confess, not usually in these rooms,' he said, 'though perhaps once or twice by post. What do you think of the problem then?'

'Rather a foolhardy indiscretion for a man in such a position.'

'Indeed, but it's also a foolhardy indiscretion for the lady. Her revenge would come at quite the cost to herself.'

'She must think the cost is worth paying.'

'Or perhaps we simply haven't the full truth yet. Will you come tomorrow?'

'Holmes,' I vowed, easily, 'I wouldn't dream of missing it.'

'Good,' he said. 'Then we will get to the bottom of all the scandals in Bohemia.'

I could hardly concentrate on the words beneath my pen, even as Holmes began reciting his deductions about the King of Bohemia with a flourish. The very idea of it, a photograph of Irene Adler, hidden away somewhere in our rooms, made me feel unreasonably hot and irritated. That he would ask for it, and then squirrel it away, less a keepsake than a *secret* —

'If you were thinking any harder,' Holmes said suddenly, 'I imagine they would hear it all the way down in Parliament. It bothers you.'

My pen blotted as I started in surprise. 'What bothers me?'

Holmes raised a sceptical eyebrow in my direction. 'The photograph I kept of Mrs Norton.'

'You're perfectly entitled to keep what you choose,' I said, a bit more defensively than I'd have liked.

'I am,' Holmes agreed, 'yet it bothers you. I don't understand.'

'It *doesn't*,' I began firmly, but he interrupted with an exasperated, *'Watson,'* and I knew I was caught. The blot on my paper grew, blacking the words I'd written. 'I don't know,' I finally admitted. 'You admire her.'

'You're jealous,' he said, in wry surprise. 'You needn't worry, Watson. My admiration for you, old boy, still remains unsurpassed.'

I grumbled, gratified and embarrassed. 'I'm not jealous,' I managed, but I could feel him watching as I blushed.

The accusation stuck with me long after our evening had drifted into other conversations: *jealous*. I wasn't sure whether to be more embarrassed and alarmed at having been jealous – despite my denials to Holmes – or at having been so easily caught out.

Since my marriage I'd thought my affections for Holmes had mellowed, but suddenly I was not so sure. Were my feelings still so strong that I was in danger of being indiscreet? Could Holmes read that old inclination in me even now, when I returned each night to home and wife?

I took a deep breath. There was no reason to think that Holmes was accusing me of any unusual attachment. So I had been jealous at his admiration of a woman – hadn't he admitted freely that his admiration for me was unparalleled? Yet I doubted he were lying awake in his room, pondering the implications. I was being ridiculous.

Still, it made my heart ache, my stomach sick, to imagine him in love with her, even as terror at my own failings settled as a hard knot of panic in my chest.

She was gone, I reminded myself. The only dangers here were the ones of my own making, and yet I knew that when it came to Sherlock Holmes, I was always going to be coming back.

'John?'

I froze, my glass halfway to my mouth, blinking with the realisation that it was not the first time Mary had said my name. 'Sorry,' I said, putting on an appropriately contrite tone. 'I'm sorry, I lost myself for a moment.'

Mary smiled. 'I was asking whether your dinner was all right.'

I looked down at my meal; I'd barely touched it. 'Oh! Yes – I

THE WATCHES OF THE NIGHT

suppose I'm just not as hungry as I expected,' I said quickly. Mary's eyes narrowed for a moment, as though she was waiting for me to say something more, but eventually she nodded and picked up the conversation again.

I could not follow her words, in much the same way I had not paid attention to the meal. My mind was not at the dinner table; it was back at Baker Street, on the case Holmes had begun that morning. 'A fascinating little problem,' he had called it. 'I should be very glad of your help.'

But the dinner arrangements had already been made, and Mary had already been put off once this week. My hands were tied. Holmes had agreed I ought to go, but his eyes had been downcast as I left him.

I should have stayed, I thought, but I smiled dutifully across at Mary and tried not to appear too bored.

If *A Study in Scarlet* was met with moderate success in *Beeton's*, the publication of *The Sign of Four* made Holmes a minor celebrity. He was furious.

'I am a consulting detective,' Holmes cried, pacing my foyer. I'd rarely seen him so agitated. 'I rely on my ability to pass unseen! How can I go unnoticed when you're publishing *this*?' He shook a copy of *Lippincott's Monthly* at me.

'You didn't protest this much the first time! You've always said I could do as I liked!'

He sighed, and his pacing stopped. 'I don't need the recognition,' he said softly, as if it were his last lifeline in a changing world, and suddenly I understood: he didn't *want* the recognition.

There is, after all, some safety in obscurity. There is some comfort in the shadows, and though Holmes was a gentleman, he did not bother with social expectations. He did not marry; he didn't have a club. He was a Bohemian, isolated by choice, and I had most certainly exposed him.

I stepped forward, easing the magazine from his hand and taking him by the elbow, leading him into the parlour. 'Come with me,' I soothed.

'Come, and we'll have tea, and I shall tell you of all the wonderful letters of praise and admiration I have received on your behalf.'

'I wonder,' Holmes said, picking through the contents of a lady's dressing table. 'I wonder.'

No longer quite so upset with me, he had asked me on an unusual case: a gentleman poisoned at his own dinner table, with only his wife in attendance. The late Mr Charles Mattox was not a man without enemies, by all accounts, but the distance poison gave to a murderer made the case difficult.

'You wonder?' I prompted. I'd been spending more of my evening hours with Holmes of late, and even a few of my days; the doctor next to my practice was quite willing to take on a patient or two when I was needed elsewhere. Though Holmes had been in a bad way for a while, it seemed the more I came, the less he was inclined to lose himself into the fugue of his cocaine; he seemed to make an effort to have some little problem on for me to assist him with. I was delighted.

'I wonder if a poison could have been concealed as a lady's cosmetics,' he said. 'What sort of husband was he?'

I remembered the lady, white with shock but not necessarily distraught. There'd been a bruise around her left wrist, mostly hidden by her sleeve. 'She didn't say, but I would think him a brute.'

'Any idea what this is?' Holmes asked, holding up one of the little cosmetic tins.

I shook my head. 'Mary uses some of these, but I wouldn't be able to tell one from another.'

'I admit I have not devoted myself to the study of cosmetics,' Holmes went on, unscrewing the lid and examining the reddish powder within. 'I shall have to remedy that immediately.'

And then he dipped his finger into the powder, and put it in his mouth.

'Holmes!' I cried, reaching already to draw his hand back, but the effect of whatever was in the tin was instantaneous. He paled, and his next breath stopped short; his eyes widened, his mouth opened, his hands jerked. 'Holmes!'

There is a trick we soldiers learned in the Indian subcontinent, when attempting to determine whether a plant was poisonous, or whether some meat had gone bad. I'll not repeat the details, but suffice it to say that it was the work of a quick moment to induce vomiting, and never mind the lady's carpet.

'You absolute fool,' I declared, even as Holmes was holding out the cosmetics tin for me to take. I shoved it at the chest of the nearest policeman in return for a porcelain washing basin. 'Get it all up, and next time try to hit the bowl.'

'Watson?'

I huffed, turning away from the door of my room so as not to see him standing there, vulnerable in dressing gown and candlelight. It had been too late to go home, but still I regretted staying. My heart had not stopped pounding. 'Not tonight, Holmes.'

'I came to apologise.'

'No, you didn't,' I snapped, unable to stop myself glancing back with a withering look. 'You came to pretend to apologise so that I'd forgive you, and I'm not going to.'

Holmes' face, nearly skeletal in the dying light, remained utterly smooth. 'You're upset,' he said, 'but you must see that it was necessary.'

I glared at him. 'You've rehearsed this, haven't you? You aren't even listening to me.' I could not remember the last time I'd been this angry with him. 'What if it had been *me* in danger, and you were the one watching me do something so stupid?'

To his credit, Holmes actually seemed to consider it. 'If it were for the case,' he said, 'I'd have understood.'

It was probably meant as reassurance, but it felt more like dismissal: my own unimportance writ large. Resentment flooded me that he could so easily prioritise even a hypothetical case over me while I could never over him.

'Yes,' I conceded, suddenly exhausted. 'That, at least, I can believe.'

It was several weeks before I felt truly comfortable again. Though I'd always known Holmes to be reckless with his own well-being – had I not noticed it, the very first time we met? Had I not known it, every time he had reached for that damned Moroccan case? – it was quite something else to watch him willingly do something that would immediately result in his death.

The space underneath my breastbone ached for days, and I struggled with the feeling of not being able to catch my breath. I should have locked myself away with Mary or with my work, but instead over the following weeks I often found myself heading out well after nightfall, anxious to check on Holmes and see that he'd not poisoned himself again, or fallen into a fire, or taken some grievous injury.

He made no mention of my agitation, if he noticed it. He would settle me in my usual chair by the fire, occasionally offering a pipe, sometimes tea, and recount his latest adventure.

If I had worried before that the distance of my marriage would irrevocably ruin our friendship, in these weeks those fears were laid to rest. Now that we had both settled in our new routines, we were, I found happily, as intimate and devoted as we had always been.

'What are you writing over there? One of ours?'

It was only a matter of time, I thought. Holmes had been without a proper case all week, making do with only a handful of trite, unimportant clients, and had finally reached his intellectual limit for the general population.

That is to say, he was bored.

'You don't mind?' I asked carefully. 'I doubt it'll be printable for many years.'

Holmes raised himself from his supine position on the sofa to peer over at me. 'The Holland family? Not sure you should be writing that one down yet,' he scolded teasingly. 'Things written down are always subject to discovery, as you know.'

'It's only a few notes for myself. I should hate to forget the details before they're beyond use.'

'You're terrible with details.' Another dull thud from the sofa:

he'd flung himself back down rather petulantly onto the cushions. 'But – no. I don't mind.'

I smiled to myself. After his protest of *The Sign of Four*, he had calmed considerably, perhaps soothed by the praise and business recognition it brought, and I already had his permission to publish a few short stories of our lesser cases. 'Recall it for me, then,' I suggested. 'Make sure I have the details right.'

Holmes snorted, but after another moment passed, slowly, theatrically, he began.

CHAPTER EIGHT

IN THE SUMMER OF 1889, MARY WENT TO BRIGHTON FOR SEVERAL weeks with her good friend Mrs Cecil Forrester, and I moved back into my old rooms at Baker Street. It was a great comfort, to have a companion while she was gone – though I missed her, it was admittedly a relief to go home at the end of a long day knowing that I would be entirely at my leisure.

Holmes himself was a soothing constant; fastidious and energetic, he met with clients, attended a few violin performances as well as the odd lecture, and was quick to recommend me a new book or introduce me to a new restaurant. At first I thought perhaps he was trying to put on a good front, to show me that he too had flourished since my marriage, or to show me the benefits of staying once more with him, but I soon dismissed both ideas as being utterly outside Holmes' character.

The last week of my stay, Holmes burst in with a new client and a plan – we too would take our holiday, with a case besides. 'One last weekend before you must go back again into the ties of marriage,' he insisted, laughing, and so I agreed, and together we packed our things and set off to the countryside around Berkshire.

The manor house in front of us was dark and silent. From our position hidden in the long grasses, watching and waiting, I was beginning to grow stiff and damp. Holmes' ability to weather these lookouts, to stay still and silent for hours at a stretch, was baffling in a man so otherwise prone toward ennui.

'Stop squirming,' Holmes hissed.

'Nothing's happening,' I hissed back. 'Admit it, Holmes – we've missed him. He must've been tipped off.'

Holmes huffed but made no answer. Exasperated, I rolled over onto my back, ignoring the house. Perhaps I could at least manage a little sleep while Holmes watched nothing happen.

After a moment, though, the grasses crackled and shifted, and Holmes' warm shoulder pressed into mine. 'There,' he said softly, pointing with one long, thin finger at a smattering of stars. 'Cassiopeia.'

I grinned. 'Why, Holmes. You've been swotting up.'

'*Astronomy - nil,*' he quoted, with a laugh. 'It's hardly good business to advertise one's weaknesses. Proving another's misconceptions wrong, however, *is.* I have taken advantage.'

'Show me, then. What else have you learned to prove me wrong?'

'The constellations,' Holmes murmured. His voice was close against my ear. 'The stars.' His long hands gestured toward the sky, as though directing the heavens, and my heart, having been quiet for so long, leapt into beating.

I could not sleep.

It was hardly the first time Holmes and I had shared a room on a case – it wasn't even the first time we had shared a bed, though we hadn't since I'd married. Space was priced for scarcity in these old country inns, and Holmes was not always flush with cash. Needs must, after all, and nothing suspicious ever had come out of this decrepit manor house.

But something was different tonight, something that left me feeling tense and awkward. The bedsheets never warmed around our bodies; Holmes never seemed to relax in his sleep.

I studied him from across the bed. His hand laid atop the quilt between us, palm up, fingers curled. It looked like an invitation, stretched out like that: like I could reach, and he would accept my touch.

The temptation was overwhelming.

His hand was warm and dry against the pad of my finger. He did not pull away, so I dared to stroke his skin again, tracing the lines of his palm. My heart pounded; my breath caught in my throat.

I wondered what the rest of his skin might feel like.

And then: he twitched, his fingers closing around mine. I went as still and silent as I could, watching his hand around my own, and hardly dared to breathe.

'Marriage is a difficult business,' Nurse had told me once, when I was very small. 'When you are grown, you will understand.'

I had hated when adults said that, and I remembered pouting loudly as she readied everything for bed. My mother and father had been fighting again; it must have been before my mother had gotten ill, before she'd gone away to the country, but I remembered her fighting – red-eyed and furious – more than any other way. 'I shan't,' I had retorted. 'If they don't like each other, why do they live together?'

'Oh, there are many reasons a husband and wife might remain so,' Nurse had said. 'Love is only one of them.'

Had I really already known so many stories, so many romances, as to turn my head? Had my nurse, a woman memory recalled as sensible and shrewd, had a taste for fanciful tales of love? I couldn't recall. I only remembered looking up at her with the outrage only a child can manage and vowing, 'If I ever get married, I'm going to love them forever and ever.'

'I hope you do,' Nurse had answered. 'Now, what story would you like?'

I've broken my vow, I thought, but then, Nurse had been right: marriage was far more complicated than any story at a child's bedtime.

Holmes had pointed out my lack of imagination many times before, but never had I felt the lack so keenly. I should have been able to imagine what might happen, thrown back into close quarters with him for a case in the country, without the usual reminders of Mary. I should have *known* – but I hadn't, and now I was destroyed by my lack of foresight.

I knew now that I was in love with Holmes.

My feelings had outgrown their fresh spring beginnings and turned into an angry, wild thicket in my chest. Whatever small affection I had thought I could prune back with marriage and distance had run rampant with neglect, and now I was helpless against the need and the fury and the want I felt for Sherlock Holmes. To touch him, to hold him. To love him, in every way I knew how. To *know him,* in every way I did not know him yet.

The journey back to London was quiet. Holmes' one-sided conversation had long since dissipated into silence; the space between us prickled with everything that I couldn't say and that he, for once, could not guess at.

I sat in that solitude, so close to him and yet so far, and counted every passing second as yet another moment of my unending betrayal.

The fire roared, flicking and leaping over the logs, threatening to overcome the small protection provided by the screen. I sat too close, staring into its furious depths as the heat grew great enough to sting – the first suggestions of a burn.

I had never been afraid of Holmes before.

For years, his mind had delighted and surprised me; it had never occurred to me to fear his deductive powers. I remembered, in fact, our first night together in Baker Street, when he'd told me any number of truths about myself. I'd relished it then, had reveled in it, eager to be seen as only he could see me.

I had been a fool.

Now the things Holmes might see in me could condemn us both, and still I couldn't turn my thoughts from them: the shape of his hands, the curl of his mouth, his face when he slept, his eyes as he woke. His laugh and his smile and his voice, his exuberance and his sincerity. The way my heart blazed when he looked at me. The way my hands ached when he touched me, desperate to touch back.

I sat and watched the fire, wondering how it would feel to be condemned by Holmes' deductions. I imagined it would be as blistering, and as permanent, as a brand.

CHAPTER NINE

I DIDN'T HEAR FROM HOLMES AGAIN FOR SEVERAL DAYS ONCE WE'D returned to London and I to my own house, which was not so unusual that anyone noticed but myself. I was a coward and a scoundrel, and I saw my patients, sat down to dinners, and went to bed at night feeling more like an actor on the stage than a man – like I was watching my life happening around me, detached and apathetic.

Even Mary noticed something was amiss with me. I knew she was concerned that something had happened during my stay with Holmes, and it had – but not as she imagined it. She saw my listlessness, my depression, and thought I had been endangered or insulted or even summarily dismissed. Perhaps she thought that it was *Holmes* who had been endangered, and I was merely uncomfortable with worry.

Holmes *was* in danger, I thought, but not with threat of violence. The threat against him was one of desire, and it came from me.

Guilt consumed me, that I could think such a thought even as my wife cared for me, and when I went upstairs, I pulled Mary close and apologised for my distance.

'I understand,' she said, even though we both knew she didn't.

'Still,' I said, 'I'm sorry,' and I kissed her – but only briefly.

Keeping myself away from Holmes, tied up in my practice and in my household responsibilities, there was only one outlet available to me: I wrote in a frenzy, hoping that every detail of Holmes I wrote, every denouement he delivered from my pen, every black mood I assigned to him, would purge him from my veins.

I wrote about cases he'd taken on very early in our association; I wrote about cases he had taken on only months ago, before the Berkshire case, before I had polluted our friendship, as though I could cleanse myself of my unworthy thoughts if only I could recall how easily we had lived together. I reached back through my many journals, hoping to find an innocent man in our adventures, hoping to become him again.

The pages poured out of me, one after another, stories about insane wives and spymasters, missing brides and Apache raiders, warring neighbors and scattered oranges. I laughed occasionally, remembering Holmes' cleverness, his feats of wit and his penchant for teasing local inspectors before finally resolving their cases; I also sat somberly in remembrance of Holmes' reckless disregard for his own safety in the face of certain danger.

Would his recklessness extend even to me?

Yes, I thought, and I would protect him from me, even if I did so belatedly.

My isolation ended abruptly one evening some six weeks later, when there was a clatter at the door that resolved itself into the shape of Sherlock Holmes, standing in my parlour. I inhaled sharply; I had underestimated how much I'd missed him.

'Doctor Watson,' he proclaimed, 'I am in need of your help.'

Were I a stronger man, I would have made my excuses. But I was only myself, and Holmes fidgeted restlessly as he waited for my answer, as if he were nervous to hear it. 'A case?'

He nodded. 'And one that may require your revolver, if I am to settle it safely.'

I could hardly send him into peril alone! My heart beat fast and hot as I made my excuses to my wife rather than to him. I retrieved my revolver at once and joined Holmes in a cab, the night pressing in around us. Holmes recounted the facts of the case, seemingly at ease, but his occasional glances in my direction had a precarious, uncertain edge to them.

The guilt was overwhelming. To have made him unsure of

our friendship through my distance – it was cruel. That he might have suffered for my own fear and doubts was alarming, and I was determined to make him as sure of my help as he had ever been.

'I had worried,' Holmes said, once we were safely back at Baker Street, the case solved, the kidnapper apprehended, and my revolver luckily unused, 'that I would have to go on this adventure alone.'

I had just finished packing our pipes, and I handed his to him, waiting for him to take a long draw, hoping the tobacco would settle any residual nerves for both of us. 'Regretfully, I have been very busy,' I excused. 'The doctor across the hall from me has taken a leave of absence for his health and I have had his patients as well as mine. But I am here now, old boy, and I am at your service should you require it.'

It was a bold thing, to lie to Sherlock Holmes, but Holmes very rarely suspected it of me and therefore I was perhaps one of the only men in London to have ever done it successfully. He hummed, sinking back into his chair a little more. 'I thought perhaps the Berkshire case did not agree with you,' he said finally.

I looked up, but he was watching the fire, not my expression, which must have been one of surprise. 'The country doesn't suit me,' I finally managed, attempting a smile. 'But I'll follow you anywhere you have need, Holmes. Even to bloody Berkshire.'

Chapter Ten

IT WASN'T VERY OFTEN THAT I FOUND MYSELF STANDING JUST INSIDE THE door to 221 Baker Street, daunted by the seventeen steps that led up to *B*, but it had been weeks since I'd climbed them and they might as well have been mountains. I lowered myself to sit on the bottom step, promising myself to get up again in a moment.

Before I could gather myself, the front door opened again, and Holmes came in. 'Watson!' he cried, his brow creasing. 'What are you doing out here?'

I whacked the banister with my cane, sullen and embarrassed at having been caught on the stairs like an invalid. 'I'm afraid I've gone quite stiff,' I confessed. 'Just needed a moment.'

'I'm not surprised, on a night this cold.' Holmes held out a hand. 'You need your chair, not these bare steps. Let me offer you my arm.'

I hesitated, but I could not deny the help – though I didn't manage to accept it gracefully. Holmes helped me carefully up the stairs, finally depositing me, churlish and ashamed in the face of his kindness, into my chair by the inviting fire.

'Thank you,' I said by way of apology, catching Holmes' wrist before he could step away.

He smiled fondly. 'It's nothing,' he assured me. 'Let me just find you a blanket.'

'So Mr Windibank gets away, and Miss Sutherland remains honour-bound to a man that doesn't exist,' I sighed, not half as satisfied with the conclusion of the case as Holmes seemed to be.

He laughed. 'Are there not many such married women in London?' he asked. 'Women who take up with men who purport to be one fine thing – well-established, sober, upstanding fellows – and yet, after the vows are said, turn out to be something else entirely? Miss Sutherland is fortunate in her timely loss.'

The whole thing left an unsavoury taste in my mouth. 'You couldn't inform Miss Sutherland of some unfortunate accident befalling Mr Angel, or some other method by which she might be relieved of her supposed obligation?' I prodded. 'She deserves a proper chance at happiness.'

'Watson, as ever, you are the romantic,' Holmes said, but he turned thoughtful. 'An accident would not do – she would only grieve. But perhaps the revelation of a wife? That wouldn't even be untrue, and it might serve as a good reminder of my whip for Mr Windibank.'

'That would suit the situation,' I agreed, relieved that Holmes would do something to help after all. 'And if you pass the news on quickly, she will have enough time to work through the injustice of it to attend the next gasfitter's ball.'

Over-warm and drowsy from the brandy Holmes had pressed into my hand, I lounged lazily on the sofa at Baker Street and could not be bothered with anything: not with going home, not with picking up a book nor any of my papers. Holmes was experimenting at his microscope, and I was content to do nothing but watch.

It was a bit like watching a ballet, watching Holmes' long, thin fingers dancing over a pipette, a slide. He had such elegance about him, such control over his body. It was entrancing.

He tweaked some dial with those long fingers and hummed. 'Have you anything to say, Watson?' he asked idly, not looking up.

I startled, caught out. Heat rose in my cheeks. 'Just lost in thought.'

'I hope you find your way back.' The very corner of his mouth curled up. 'You seem very intent on some problem. Is it a worthwhile one?'

It is a problem of you, I thought, and it was one I was becoming less practiced at avoiding and more tempted every day to solve. What the solution might be, I could not say.

'It is only a trifle,' I answered, a bit unsteadily. Holmes looked over, eyebrow raised, and I set about distracting him. 'Take my mind off it, Holmes. Tell me about your bacteria.'

'Watson, are you quite ready? I'll not miss the beginning of this symphony – if you are not ready in two minutes, I will leave without you!'

No doubt Holmes would be as good as his word, and I hurried out into the sitting room. 'Here!' I cried, but was stopped dead at the sight of him waiting for me.

He was a vision in formal full-dress: black jacket nipping in at his trim waist, emphasised by the deep lapels drawing downward and the low cut of his waistcoat. He looked sharp, but soft to the touch, and somehow he seemed miles long; for a moment I was overcome by an urge to press Holmes' torso into the cup of my palms, to see how it might fit.

'The cab is here,' Holmes said, interrupting my thought. 'Don't forget your scarf. The night is cold.'

I seized upon the opportunity to disappear into my old room – still mine by Holmes' generosity – and gather myself. How would I get through the night, sitting next to him? So close, and yet unable to touch him? The prospect was torturous. His wrists, his shoulders! It was impossible to contemplate.

I shook myself, wrapped my scarf too firmly around my neck. If I could not control myself tonight, I would be the ruin of us both.

There had been another man once, long ago. A boy, really. When I was very young and very foolish, as most university boys are, there had been a tall, dark student with a flop of hair and a smile that lit up the night, and I had fancied myself in love.

'What do you think will happen to us?' I had dared to ask him once. My examinations had been nearly finished; his had been over for days. He would be leaving school at the end of the year, off to join some government office with his father; I didn't imagine I would ever see him again. It wasn't the sort of friendship a man retained – it was the sort of friendship a man pretended he had never had.

'Mm. Someday we'll grow out of it,' he said, understanding my true question. 'We'll each go off and marry some pretty young thing and forget about all this. Act offended when it gets brought up in some club or another. That's the way of things, Watson.'

I hummed. I knew that was the future I would someday embrace, for society and survival if nothing else. I only hoped I would find happiness in it as easily as he expected.

I was not as sure of it as I wished I could be.

Holmes was in good spirits by the time we returned to Baker Street, having ensnared a would-be murderer working in the guise of an occultist. The suspect had secured his invitation to an exclusive party by advertising an expertise in palmistry, intending to kill his prey during a reading; Holmes had stopped him just as the knife was drawn.

'Palmistry,' Holmes scoffed, throwing off his coat. 'Of all the foolish things.'

'You don't believe in any of the occultist practices then, Holmes?' I asked innocently, but at Holmes' severe look I dissolved into laughter. 'Come now – you yourself can tell a great many things about a person by the look of their hands.'

'But not their futures. Here – ' Holmes darted forward and grasped my hand in his own, turning it over. His touch was warm and sure. 'There are implications in your calluses, of course, and in your fingernails, in your steadiness of hand, but they only gain meaning if I see you as a whole. These lines' – he drew a fingertip slowly up my palm – 'are only a minuscule detail in the entire portrait of you.'

He looked up. I had never seen his eyes so closely before; they were wide and surprised, and I could see now that their piercing grey was feathered with a light, unexpected blue.

Holmes was asleep at his desk when I next stopped in at Baker Street, having kept myself away for nearly a month. I sighed, the usual exhaustion I felt after an evening at my club coming second to the affection and the warmth and the calm I so often felt in those rooms.

Quietly, I banked the fire, eased the pen from Holmes' grasp, and draped a shawl over his shoulders. If I thought I could chivvy him to bed, I would have, but Holmes was a notoriously light sleeper when he was fixated on a problem, and nothing was a better indicator of such a fixation than working himself to collapse. If I attempted to move him now, he would only wake and insist on resuming his work.

There was a smudge of ink on Holmes' face, near his mouth, where his head must have fallen against the papers before turning in his sleep. I touched a finger to it – it was already dry. His skin there was soft, and I thought about what it would be like to put my mouth to that spot. Whether it would mark, as obvious as the ink.

I should have jerked myself away. I should have fled.

Instead I lingered, sick with horror at myself, and brushed the hair back from his brow.

Just a few days later I was apologising to Mary, holding up Holmes' note as I rose from the dinner table. 'It does seem to be a matter of some urgency.'

'No trouble at all,' she smiled. 'I know well the importance of Mr Holmes' work. Pass on my regards, would you? And invite him to dinner, John? Goodness only knows how often he finishes a meal himself.'

It would have been better had she protested, I thought, as I kissed her cheek and left the table. It would have been easier, perhaps, if she had held me tighter, refused to let me go; if she'd demanded my attention and my presence the same way Holmes did. If she could command my heart.

The night air was not nearly cold enough to douse such thoughts as I set off toward Baker Street. Of course I could not blame Mary for my wandering gaze, this I knew. Of course I couldn't lament her understanding, nor her willingness to maintain a household without conflict.

And I did love her, didn't I? Didn't I feel relief to come home to her at night? Didn't I feel desire, and comfort, and protectiveness toward her?

I did, I thought, but these were damning, dishonourable thoughts, and it wasn't quite enough to absolve me of my blame.

Thus I resolved very early on to spend all of Christmas Day at home, entertaining with the Forresters and several others of Mary's good friends. I'd never quite got on well with the group of them – none of their gentlemen had served in the war, as I had, and most leaned instead toward government officers or businessmen. My association with Holmes had done me little good in such company; I could see their offices' secrets in their cuffs and shoes and the states of their hats, yet I had little empathy for them.

But I was resolved, because every instinct in me was that I should escape to Baker Street instead. The Christmases Holmes and I had had were always very quiet and uneventful – he was never one for wassailing, obviously – but they were calm, cosy days that drifted into evenings slowly, aided at the end by Mrs Hudson's skills with a fattened goose. It was the quintessential example of the domesticity we had enjoyed once, and with my own home filled with guests and games and wassail punch, I longed for it more than ever.

That was a dangerous longing, though, and I put Holmes out of my mind and went to head the Christmas table, Mary at my side, smiling with good cheer but surrounded by bores and bureaucrats.

I did not see Holmes until the second morning after Christmas, and it had felt too long, too separated from the celebrations. I told Mary I intended to see to a few patients and slipped out.

He had a case, and my heart swelled to see him, to spend a moment or two watching him as he studied some ill-used hat upon a chair. His brow was furrowed in concentration and a sense of peace settled over me, as though stepping into the room had fitted me back into my proper place.

There had been no real crime, he explained. 'Only one of those whimsical little incidents which will happen when you have four million people all jostling each other within the space of a few square miles. Amid the action and reaction of so dense a swarm of humanity, every possible combination of events may be expected to take place, and many a little problem will be presented which may be striking and bizarre without being criminal.'

I wondered if Holmes would find me striking, if he knew what was in my heart, and the next day when he let our jewel thief go, I wondered if he would commute *my* felony, too. Would he condemn me, if he knew? Or would he simply relegate me to the bizarre?

CHAPTER ELEVEN

'WATSON!'

Time slowed. I could hear the tick of my watch in my pocket, the scratch of a rat running through the alley. A breeze washed over me, a jolt rushed through me, and from somewhere only a foot or two away and yet miles off, Holmes was shouting my name, reaching for me – but I was already falling.

How odd, I thought, watching his eyes widen, watching his hands spread, *how very afraid he looks. It's only a counterfeiter. It's only a little knife. Isn't it?*

'Watson!'

Yes, I recognised that look of utter terror. I had seen it many times before in my own mirror as I thought of him, tugging uselessly on the knot under my breastbone, the one that would lead me to him no matter where we each two were. To see it now on his face, to see my own desperation and sorrow and need reflected back at me, was the most wretched thing I could ever have imagined. *I'm all right Sherlock*, I wanted to say, but I could find neither the breath nor the words to speak.

'*Watson! – John!*'

And then: I hit the ground, hard. I'd forgotten it was coming. I just had time to look up and think, distantly, that I could see the stars tonight, and then everything went black.

He was there when I woke.

The pain was there too, as well as the tell-tale nausea of morphine. I gasped against it, but a cool hand slipped into mine, steadying me.

'You are at Baker Street,' he said, low and even. 'And your injuries were not severe, thank God, but do not strain them now, when I have worked so hard to keep them clean.'

I laughed; my throat was dry and dusty, and my shoulder flared into searing pain where the blade had met my flesh. Not severe though, he'd said. I trusted him.

'You foolish man,' Holmes went on, and here his voice strained into anger. 'To just – let him stab you like that. You stupid, foolish man. *Stop laughing,* you'll hurt yourself.'

He lifted a cup of lukewarm tea to my mouth, insistent. It was too sweet – his own cup, then – but I drank greedily of it anyway, watching him. He was disheveled, his hair wild. His hand, where it was caught in mine, was trembling.

And the look on his face: my breath caught, but I knew that look. I knew that concern, that tenderness, that heartache and devotion and need.

It was an impossible thing, an unbelievable thing, but the more I watched him, fussing over me, the more certain of it I became.

I drifted in and out of consciousness for the next day, but eventually I became aware again, and it was not Holmes' gentle touch nor soft voice that tugged me toward the surface.

It was Mary.

I stiffened in the bed when I recognised her, feeling distinctly caught out – in Holmes' own bed! – before my wound made itself known again and I forced myself to relax. 'John,' she whispered, a little tearfully. 'John, there you are. I'm so glad to see you wake.'

'What time is it?' I asked, but she shushed me almost immediately, nodding to the other side of the bed, where Holmes was curled up in a chair and fast asleep.

'He's only just dropped off,' she explained, still whispering, 'and I fear he looks nearly as bad as you do. It's half-nine, if you must know. Do you think you could manage some broth?'

I nodded, not taking my eyes off Holmes' contorted frame, his exhausted face. Mary checked my wound and cleaned my face of sweat, and finally I looked back at her. 'You don't have to,' I murmured.

She shook her head. 'If you're to convalesce here, I must take care of you when I can,' she declared quietly. 'Now let me put this pillow behind you – here comes Mrs Hudson with the broth.'

Holmes was sitting by the fire when I emerged from my room. Shadows played upon his thin face, making him look gaunt, and exhausted, and somehow fragile, sitting alone there, in the dark. The longing I had grown so used to suddenly seemed unbearable, and now I knew that he felt that ache, too.

I took a deep breath, and risked everything. 'You care for me.'

Holmes did not look up. He did not move, yet something about him seemed to crumple, to cave. 'Of course,' he murmured, staring into the blaze. 'We are very close friends, aren't we?'

'That's not what I meant,' I said, as softly as I could. Holmes stiffened in his chair. 'I mean something deeper. Something you have tried to deny.'

The fire crackled and popped into the silence. 'I've no idea what you mean,' he said finally.

Slowly, carefully, I went to him, placed my hand upon his arm, knelt beside him so I might see his face. 'Holmes. Look at me.' There were, to my infinite surprise, tear tracks on his cheeks. I dared to reach up, to take his face in my hands. To brush his tears away. 'I care for you that way too.'

He stared and stared, but just when I gathered the courage to lean in, he drew himself back.

'I am not wrong about this, Holmes, and I cannot live this way.' I paced the floor at Baker Street, distraught; he looked unfairly calm, standing at the window with his violin, staring out into the night. I'd interrupted him in the middle of a song, burst into argument before he could stop, and now the strains of a melancholy tune were companion to my distress.

'And yet we must do nothing.'

'Nothing? Holmes, I *love* – '

The bow fell from the strings with a screech. 'No, don't say it,' he said, finally turning to me. His eyes were rimmed with red, the bags underneath drawn deep. I ached to look at him. 'You mustn't. I won't make an adulterer of you, John Watson, and I'm criminal enough already without your sin on my hands.'

I wanted to kiss that sin into his very skin. I wanted to throttle his sin out of him and into myself. 'Do you think me innocent of those same crimes?' I hissed, enraged. 'Do you think I spoke without knowing the consequences of these things I have tried so hard to deny? That I did not choose to accept them?'

'You may accept them,' Holmes said quietly, 'but I will not.' And before I could respond, he turned away and, once more, lifted his bow.

Perhaps a man in my position should have run. Perhaps I should've turned my back to 221 Baker Street, never again to darken its door; perhaps I should have taken the grace Holmes offered me and gone home to lose myself in the sanctified love of my virtuous wife. Perhaps I, having spent so many years with Holmes putting criminals in the docks already, should have taken every chance to avoid ending up there myself.

I did not.

I had seen the naked emotion in Holmes' eyes, and I *could* not.

Holmes, for his part, seemed insistent on behaving as though nothing had changed. He still took my visits, accepted and even asked for my assistance, returned my messages and passed his regards on to Mary, though the last did become more pointed as the days drifted by.

But he wasn't unaffected. He stopped stealing my biscuits or packing my pipe, and when next he appeared out of some dark alley after scuffling with some fiend, blood dripping from his brow, he dodged me entirely and instead he'd staunch the bleeding with a handkerchief, refusing to let me see.

Yet he did not turn me away. He didn't ask that I not come.

And his eyes followed me whenever I had to leave, with a familiar pain writ upon his brow.

For weeks we wandered around each other in this daze, knowing and pretending otherwise, recognising in each other the things we had each tried to hide in ourselves. But it was a façade, and facades, inevitably, must collapse.

I knew it first. We'd been running, first chasing, then escaping – our feet flew on the wet streets of London, step in step, stride in stride – and by the time we clattered up the stairs inside Baker Street, breathless and surging with adrenalin, I knew.

I closed the door behind us. Holmes stood silhouetted by the fire, his hands hanging uselessly by his side as he watched me. 'I cannot,' he said, apropos of nothing. 'I refuse.'

I only looked at him.

'I *will* not,' Holmes said then. His voice betrayed his determined declaration.

'I don't mean to force you,' I said softly. 'I don't ask for what you resolve not to give. But I think you already know that you will, just as I know that I will.' I sighed and ran a hand through my hair, feeling myself shake as my courage strengthened. 'We can't go on like this, Holmes. Every second I'm with you, we move inexorably closer. But I will not go, and you will not send me away. You know whatever resolve we had has already been broken.'

'We agreed,' Holmes repeated uselessly, even as he took a step closer to me. 'We agreed.'

I was shaking; I could feel it in my hands, in my knees, in the insides of my elbows. I was going to touch him. He was walking toward me, stumbling almost – as though he were trying to resist, and couldn't. The sight made my breath short, made my cheeks hot. 'We didn't,' I countered, huffing a nervous laugh as my hands clenched around themselves, restraining myself. 'I've always – ' My voice faded against the words I had for so long prevented myself from saying, and I had to try again. 'I have always wanted you.'

'You were the one who left,' he said, breathless, and suddenly he was there, standing in front of me in pale, trembling, uncertain glory. 'You set the limitation yourself.'

'I thought I was protecting you,' I said. He was so close I could smell the lingering scent of his tobacco, could see the barest suggestion of a day's worth of whiskers on his jaw.

Holmes' eyes were sharp under his brow, and something like joy seemed to rise in them even as I watched, fiery and fierce. 'I don't need protection from you,' he said, and then his mouth was on mine, and I was consumed in the blaze.

Together we drowned in firelight.

In all my imaginings, I could never have imagined this: the graze of hands, of mouths, of teeth, the stretch of Holmes' neck and the gasp of his voice, the beat of his heart and the flush of his blood. The unveiling of a thin chest, a dusting of hair, a peak of a nipple. The shape of his mouth, breathless and bewildered – the heat of his tongue, seeking and searching.

He clutched at me, arched into me, his every façade crumbling around my feet like so much discarded linen, and I could have wept for the beauty of it.

We fumbled at each other, coming undone at every new sensation, every brush of skin against undiscovered skin, pushing and pulling each other closer. The dying fire gilded over every plane and curve of Holmes' flesh, and I ran my tongue along each rise and fall, eager to taste him. The first touch of our pricks together was a revelation; the first thrust of our hips together was an epiphany.

I found his eyes with mine, desperate that he know, that he see, that he *understand,* and then he said my name against my mouth, a prayer and a benediction both, and together we thrust, together we surged – and together, we fell, into complete, devastating bliss.

Holmes and I had just settled into a relaxed, comfortably smug silence, when the bell rang downstairs. Our eyes met from across the sitting room as tension whipped through us, the risk of our shared secret suddenly heightened under the eye of a client.

It was even worse than that, however: it was Tobias Gregson of Scotland Yard.

I clenched my hands to hide their trembling and stood, making my excuses, but Holmes stopped me with a touch to my shoulder that I felt all the way down to my spine. 'We shall do it together, Watson,' he said, falsely jovial, 'or I shall not do it at all.'

He'd stood with his back to the good inspector so that I might see the truth in his eyes, I realised. They pleaded with me to stay – to not make him face this fear alone.

But Gregson did not notice anything amiss. He sat on our sofa and recounted his story, looking back and forth between us, watching us, and did not notice.

Cautiously, my disquiet eased into relief, and when Gregson finally left, Holmes gathered me to him and kissed me soundly. 'I thought we were done for,' I confessed.

He laughed. 'Gregson isn't a bad detective,' he said, 'but perhaps it is just as well that he's not any better.'

We burst into the flat, panting with the victorious giddiness of a crime solved and a murderer caught swelling in our chests. We had chased our man throughout the streets and alleys of London, driving him into the path we'd laid and finally into all the ready teeth of Scotland Yard. It had been fierce, and frenzied, and *brilliant*.

I shut the door behind us, vibrating with energy, and when I turned back to the room, Holmes was there.

For a moment I could only stare, struck still and silent by the intensity of his gaze as lust flashed up my spine. His cheeks were flushed with exhilaration; his eyes were shining with need.

It was only three steps to him.

We crashed together, ripping the collars from each other's necks and the buttons from each other's waistcoats in our rush. Holmes pushed at my jacket, my trousers, shoving me back against the door; I dragged him with me, steadying us as we rocked together. He groaned and shoved some more, seeking *skin*, and I bared it for him, bared myself to him, sinking into the heat of his mouth.

'John,' he whispered, with that mouth, that reverential, devoted, *needy* mouth, and I tipped back my head and let him shatter me with it, with every lick and suck and bite.

Chapter Twelve

As soon as the weather turned fair again, Mary set off for the coast.

'Oh, I hate to leave you again so early in the season,' she fretted, the night before her train was due to depart. She'd developed a cough in the last few days, though, and I was sure the milder weather at the coast would help. 'But you'll be all right, I'm sure?'

'I will,' I promised. 'I have my patients to keep me busy, of course, and I'll be able to catch up a little on my writing. Holmes has been running me ragged on our latest case – ' which was, of course, a fabrication we'd invented to excuse my absences – 'and I'm afraid my editor is becoming a little worked up.'

Mary laughed. 'I shall have to send Mr Holmes a letter, then,' she said, teasing, 'and ask him to give you some peace.'

The idea of Holmes receiving such a letter turned my stomach cold, but I tried to summon an appropriate smile. 'I'll pass on the message to him,' I said, and Mary looked up from where she was packing up her needlework to smile back, before coming over to kiss my cheek.

'Will you miss me?' she asked playfully.

'Yes,' I said, more lie than truth, and had to swallow the truth back.

'Tell me about this one.'

My fingertips skated over a ripple of puckered flesh on Holmes' shoulder, a silvery-pink mark that nearly glowed in the dim light of the lamp. He was stretched out on his stomach, letting me examine every inch of skin, every scar.

There were more of them than I had thought there would be.

'Mm. The docks. Wapping. The sailor was just a petty thief, and he wasn't as committed to using the knife as he thought he was.'

I pressed a kiss to it, breathing warm and slow against Holmes' skin. Sherlock's skin. I imagined I could feel the beat of his heart through his ribcage, and let my lips rest against it. 'You have been reckless, old boy.'

He shifted, rolled over so he could catch my head in both hands and bring our mouths together, gently, reassuringly. 'You know I'm perfectly able to defend myself.'

'I know, or you would not be here today. It's the possibility that itches under my skin. The prospect that some day, one of us will outlive the other.'

'Hush.' Sherlock kissed the words away. 'It is a mistake to theorize without all the facts. Perhaps we'll die together, in the fire of glory.'

'You'll never die,' I countered determinedly, and pressed him back down against the bed.

Sherlock Holmes had a particularly lovely prick, I thought, hollowing my cheeks around it. He had particularly lovely hips, too, and particularly lovely thighs. He was lovely where his belly trembled, and where the flush began somewhere above his navel, and where it spread up and up, up his chest and his neck and into his cheeks, into the swollen lip caught between his teeth to keep his sighs from fully forming into the moans and pleas they longed to be.

'John,' Sherlock whispered, and his voice was filled with reverence and awe even though I was the one on my knees. One hand cupped the back of my head as the other scrabbled along the table for something to grip. His breath stuttered in, in, and out, out, out. '*John.*'

I did not answer, but sucked a little harder and pressed my tongue against his flesh, savouring the feeling of it. I hoped he could deduce the things I meant to say with the way my mouth was achingly full, with the way I held his hips and the way I swallowed around his cockhead: *I will love you, if you'll let me. I will adore you.*

I knew Sherlock heard me from the way he quaked and gasped and spent into my mouth. I knew he adored me back.

'You're thinking too loudly,' Holmes said, interrupting my wonderings as to whether Mrs Hudson had left sandwiches up for us. One long, thin finger, too cold in the night air, found its place against my lips, and I kissed it because it was there, and because it would make Holmes blush. 'You are meant to be watching our suspect's door, not considering the state of your dinner.'

'Perhaps if I'd had dinner,' I whispered, lips still pressed against Holmes' finger, breathing warm against the skin, 'I could be more focused on the door.'

'If you'd had dinner, you'd be half-asleep in front of the fire, instead of preparing to catch a serial blackmailer.' Holmes' eyes, when they cut to mine, were merry in the dark, teasing and affectionate. 'The sandwiches will keep for you.'

His finger still had not moved, however, so I took advantage of the distraction I posed and captured it between my lips, pulling it deep into my mouth to warm it. Holmes' breath drew in sharp, but he didn't move away until I released him. 'You're cold,' I opined, 'and as hungry as I am, though perhaps not for sandwiches. How sure are you that our man is here?'

Holmes shifted. 'Not sure enough,' he said finally, and pushed me, laughing, back against the alley brick.

'What is it you're reading, Watson?'

Holmes had flung himself dramatically onto the settee, throwing one arm over his forehead. His experiment, which had occupied him all day but had now been summarily abandoned, had clearly not gone the way he would have liked. I hid my affectionate smile behind my novel.

'One of Eliot's,' I answered. 'I doubt you'd care for it, though.'

He hummed in consideration. 'Read it aloud a little,' he requested. 'Perhaps it would do me good to not care about something for a while.'

I obliged, making my voice soft and steady to soothe Holmes' disappointments. With the fire crackling in the grate and the light fading into the night, the room felt warm and cosy, and I had not read more than a few lines before I inadvertently discovered the true reason Holmes had been struggling with his experiment: exhaustion. Laid out on the sofa, he was already asleep, his breath slow and even in his chest, his mouth gone soft and sweet.

I trailed off, content for the moment to watch him sleep. It was unusual to see him without his energy, without the presence of his ambition and curiosity. He looked younger, and somehow more fragile, too.

'John?' Holmes mumbled. 'Still there?'

'Still here, Sherlock,' I assured him, and returned to my book.

'Have you ever?' I said, soft and low, slipping my hand beneath Holmes' body to trace over the swell of his buttocks, to draw a suggestion over the space between them.

There was a moment of hesitation, and then he said, 'Yes,' the word punching out of him. There was eagerness in him, in the twitch of his cock and the tremble of his belly, but there was also a layer of anxiety and embarrassment – something I had never heard before in our bed.

I wanted to tread carefully, and spent a moment or two licking softly at his cockhead, soothing some of his tension out of him while my fingers played over the crease in his arse. 'Did you enjoy it?'

He gasped and covered his face with his hands. 'Yes. Oh God, John.' Under my tongue, his prick hardened even further, a pearl of fluid appearing at the tip.

Oh, I realised, not anxiety at all, but a different sort of tension: anticipation. *Craving.* I finally slipped my fingers down into the warm space between his arse cheeks, seeking the furled muscle there, rubbing over it gently, and watched, stunned with arousal, as Holmes gasped and cried out, grinding himself down hard against me, and then, suddenly, unexpectedly, spent himself completely at only the barest suggestion of a breach.

I was nearly asleep when Mary slid across the bed, pressing herself against me. Her initial intention was clear, but I kept my answering touch light and chaste as I wrapped an arm around her, and eventually she subsided.

'You're very quiet lately,' she said. Her voice was deliberately even, as though she had already reasoned any anger away. I kissed her temple.

'Between my patients and Holmes' clients, I barely have a moment's rest,' I deflected, equally as deliberate.

She hummed, and her tone turned discerning. 'You certainly have been particularly busy with Mr Holmes lately.'

Mary was a bright, intuitive woman, I knew, with incredible strength of will and a perceptive eye, and I had not forgotten that she was the sort of woman who would engage a detective if she were truly mystified. I knew I would have to be careful in order to deceive her fully, yet the thought of deceiving her at all filled me with guilt and discomfort.

I had no desire to hurt her, even as I succumbed to the desires that betrayed her.

'I'll try to spend more time at home,' I promised, though I was sure I would break that promise entirely. I laid awake all night, thinking about the conflict I had created, wondering if I could ever find a balance.

CHAPTER THIRTEEN

MARY AND I DID NOT ATTEND VERY MANY PARTIES, BUT EVERY SO OFTEN there was one I simply could not avoid. By the time I had delivered her back home and set out for Baker Street, it was hideously late – nearly two in the morning – but I hadn't seen Holmes in days.

I could see from the street that 221B was dark and quiet, but I let myself in nonetheless. Moonlight streamed in from the open curtains, illuminating the empty chairs, the cold fireplace. The violin was set on the table, abandoned. The dark made the room feel deserted, neglected – an ancient ruin built of books and papers.

I made my way to Holmes' bedroom, and was relieved to see the familiar curve of a body under the bedcovers, to hear the soft susurrus of breath. He was awake, I could tell – he was breathing light and soft, not in the deep, even way he did in sleep – but he didn't turn to me.

I shed my shoes and my jacket and slipped, fully dressed, under the covers behind him, wrapping an arm over his ribs. 'I've missed you,' I whispered into the shell of his ear.

He did not answer. Instead he found my hand in the dark, his fingers winding in mine, holding me closely, keeping me tightly bound.

The storm raged over London, thunder and lightning rattling against the windowpanes. The city cowered under its force, and I claimed my room again in Baker Street to weather it out, blaming my sore leg and achy shoulder for being unable to move comfortably under the winds and gusts of rain.

It should have been a luxury, to spend so many days at once with

Holmes without any need for excuse. To wake up in the drizzling mornings and see him soft and rumpled at the breakfast table, and to while away the rainy afternoons, exchanging quiet glances and the occasional laugh. To let the days wash themselves into evenings, into nights, and never have to wonder about the time.

It should have been the perfect taste of life lived side-by-side. Instead it was only playacting.

The risk of our secret lost its dark appeal under the constant onslaught of things we could not do or say, the ways in which we had to censor ourselves, and I could see the impermanence of my stay begin to wear on Holmes as the spectre of my eventual departure filled the space between us. He looked at me as though I were already gone; I felt his gaze so heavily upon my heart I thought it might even leave a bruise.

That evening Sherlock was particularly beautiful, stretched out on the sofa. I told him I thought so, matter of factly, then leaned over to prove it to him with a kiss, pressing him down into the cushions as softness slowly gave way to crushing heat.

We were both distracted enough that neither of us heard the pull of the bell, and it wasn't until Mrs Hudson was knocking on our door as she cracked it open that I realised the danger, and then I startled away so fast I nearly fell to the floor.

Holmes, for his part, immediately set about coughing, one hand clapped over his mouth. 'Mrs Hudson,' I exclaimed with authority, catching on to his game, 'I need a hot compress and a pot of tea immediately. I have just examined him, and Mr Holmes is coming down with a cold.'

'Oh, dear,' she said, her hands fluttering. The client she'd brought up peered around her curiously. 'But he seemed so well earlier.'

I placated her as best I could, gave instructions to get the client's name, and finally pushed the door closed behind her before turning back to Holmes. 'I'm so sorry,' I said.

He raised himself from the sofa, shaking his head. His hands were trembling. 'It's all right,' he said. 'We are both to blame.'

The next night I set off for Baker Street with the adrenalin still heavy in my veins. I had had several false starts – first, like a habit, telling Mary that I'd had a message from Holmes at my practice, requesting my presence, and then, suddenly, changing my mind and telling her I was too tired to go, before changing it once again and making an excuse of having expected another message and received none. She accepted each lie in turn with an ease that made me ill.

London was alive outside the cab window, and I was not at all sure I wanted to be at Baker Street, but every option that presented itself was dismissed in turn; I had no desire to appear in such a rough state at my club, where my friends would surely notice my distress. Every other pub or restaurant that rose to mind carried with it such memories of Holmes that I shied away from them instinctively.

There was one place, however, I had never been with Holmes.

I pounded on the roof of the cab to get the cabbie's attention and redirected him down to the docks. Perhaps a game or two of cards would set me to rights, and I settled back, my mind made up, feeling suddenly reckless and also strangely buoyant.

In the days following Mrs Hudson's unfortunate interruption, Holmes was uncharacteristically silent and subdued. When Mary left for another weekend in the countryside, I returned once more to Baker Street, worried that his mood would turn so black that he'd seek relief in his needle.

I didn't notice any sign of the little glass bottles, however, and by Sunday evening I was able to relax enough to pull out my papers and work on another story for *The Strand*. I had just finished adding the title across the top with a flourish when Holmes leaned over my shoulder to read it. 'What's this?'

'Have a look then,' I offered, handing him the papers. I was sure I had done a neat enough job of it this time, and he would find very little to critique. 'I'll light my pipe while you read it.'

I did so, and he spent a few minutes reading the pages before handing them back without his usual, affectionate tease. 'Are you pleased at last?' I asked, trying to bait him to it.

He offered me a pale, weak smile. 'It is not inaccurate,' he admitted. 'But in the beginning – perhaps you ought to make a mention of your wife. Let us not forget that I am the only one of us who still remains a bachelor.'

It would take Holmes hours to explain everything he had discovered about our latest suspect: it was the price he paid for his brilliance. When my leg began to stiffen in my seat, he brushed a hand over my knee and told me gently to go home, and for once I couldn't argue.

Mary met me at the door, fresh from the coast, and her smile was rejuvenating. 'I didn't expect you home so early,' she said as I shed my hat and coat. 'I got your word that you would be late with Mr Holmes.'

'The case concluded earlier than anticipated.' Her good mood was catching, and I leaned in to sneak a kiss onto her cheek. 'And he had no more use for me tonight.'

We went into the parlour, where we shared a small dinner and a quiet conversation about the goings-on of the house, until finally I sat back in my chair and rubbed at my leg. 'It went stiff at Scotland Yard,' I confided, and she smiled warmly. I knew that look; I had seen it on Holmes' face many times after a case. Instinctively, my blood began to rise.

'Then let us go upstairs,' she said. She helped me to my feet, her voice coy with suggestion. 'I will call for a hot bath.'

It was a quiet evening spent at Baker Street when next I managed it, an increasingly rare occurrence as I tried to balance Holmes' and Mary's claims against one another. I sank into the pages of a novel, letting the familiar hum of our rooms wash away the stress: the rustle of Holmes' papers, the clink of his glassware, the pace of his step across the floor. The smell of smoke – I caught my thought. *Smoke?*

I looked about; there was indeed a cigarette dangling precariously from Holmes' mouth. A cloud of smoke hung about the room – I was surprised I hadn't noticed before. 'I wish you wouldn't do that quite so enthusiastically while I'm here,' I said, coughing. 'It's horrible.'

'Mm. Gotten into the habit of you being out,' Holmes returned. His tone stung, and I could see from his glowering expression that it was meant to. I ought to have realised – Holmes had been in a foul mood lately, increasingly bitter about my absences, and I should have suspected that being *quiet* did not necessarily mean being genial.

'I can't say that all these fumes entice me to come more often,' I threw back, uninterested in placating him when he behaved like this. He blew out another stream of smoke thoughtfully.

'No,' he agreed. 'How lucky for us both.'

For many months, things were steady, if not easy. Then in February of 1890, Mary took ill with a fever. I stayed home to fret alongside the staff, though Mary insisted she was fine and Holmes insisted he needed me. I'd told him quite clearly that he most certainly did not, and regretted it for days.

'It's just a lingering chill,' Mary assured me. 'Once spring comes I'll return to the coast, and be much improved.'

'The fever will have to go long before the winter does,' I said, taking a moment to listen to her lungs, fearful the sickness would move into her chest.

'The worrisome doctor,' she said, affectionate but teasing. 'What a loathsome nurse you make, John Watson.'

'As stern and unyielding as the worst sort,' I agreed.

She caught my hand as her expression softened. 'A good husband though,' she decided, her voice quiet. 'The very best. I'd recommend him to the ladies but, you see, I'm rather attached.'

My stomach lurched; my chest burned fiercely all the way up my throat. Even here, at her sickbed, I had been thinking about Holmes. 'Ah, but even great men have their weaknesses,' I warned her. 'And I'm naught but a devil.'

She laughed. 'A devil, but a beloved one,' she said. 'There's no way I'd love you better.'

We almost never had the time to come together slowly, restricted as we were to stolen moments and shadowed secrets, but tonight, finally – a week on from our petty disagreement – would be different. Mrs Hudson had gone for the weekend to the country, and Mary, having recovered from her fever, to the seaside. Without having to discuss it aloud, Sherlock and I closed up the house. Anticipation curled heavily through the air.

But by the time I had him laid out in front of the fireplace, nested in cushions and blankets stolen from anywhere we could find them, I could barely bring myself to touch him. I did not want to break through the soft, hesitant atmosphere with urgent hands and crude thrusts. I wanted to show him how it always ought to be between us, how it felt in my heart to think of him: warm and tender and everlasting.

He trembled under that slow, gentling touch. He shook and gasped, and stretched up to meet me, and when I looked down at him in the firelight, I found I had to kiss away the tears pooling beneath his eyelids, pressing my lips softly and carefully against his skin in complete adoration – pressing my devotion and my reverence into his flesh as though each kiss could be our holy benediction.

CHAPTER FOURTEEN

THE AVENUE OF CHESTNUTS LEADING TO AND FROM WISTERIA LODGE made for a dark, rather somber walk as we set off back toward town, leaving Inspector Baynes and his constable to lock up the house once again. Holmes hummed to himself here or there, but I could not shake the cold feeling of what Mr Scott Eccles must have experienced there. I shivered at the very thought.

'Are you all right?' Holmes asked, putting his hand to my forearm and stopping in the lane. 'You look nearly as pale as that constable back there.'

'Fine,' I managed. 'Only thinking how very unsettling it must have been to wake up there alone.'

Holmes' face grew serious. 'You understand the risk that Scott Eccles had taken in coming here, of course.'

I nodded, my heart heavy. 'He was like us.' I already knew this; I had known it as soon as I had seen him at Baker Street.

'Like us, yet not so lucky,' Holmes nodded. 'But we'll protect him, John. I promise you that.'

'Would that men such as us needed no protection,' I muttered.

Holmes squeezed my hand in his. 'I wish it too,' he said. 'Someday that may yet be the case.' He kissed me then, under the chestnuts, and I let him, wanting desperately to believe it could be.

The bed was huge and ornate, heaped with pillows and drapes, and as I stared across its great expanse, a trickle of fear went down my spine.

Holmes had thrown himself into a chair by the fire to review his knowledge of Nicholas Ruskin and his state of affairs, though the dilapidated manor and wild grounds were probably indication enough. I wondered how much more devastation the blackmailer would wreak on the estate if Ruskin could not find a way to supplement his income.

Looking at the bed, I thought I might suspect one way he had in mind. 'Don't you think it's odd,' I asked slowly, 'that in all this great house, there's only one room suitable for guests?'

'Not at all,' Holmes snorted. 'Given its state of repair, I'm surprised there's even that.'

I shifted, trying to sound nonchalant. 'You don't think there's any chance that Ruskin is aiming to become a blackmailer himself?'

'Ruskin's not intelligent enough,' he said dismissively, and then, as the question's true meaning caught up to him, the tiniest hint of hurt appeared between his brows. 'If you are disinclined to share a bed with me, I can make do on the floor.'

'No, of course not,' I assured him quickly, but the guilt did little to soothe the fear sharpening underneath my breast.

We'd both had far too much drink, I thought, eying the flush creeping out of Holmes' collar. Too much brandy too late at night, and we had meandered into as frank a conversation as we had ever had before. 'Have you really never?'

Holmes shook his head. 'It didn't even occur to me until after I'd left school,' he admits. 'But no – never. I suppose I'm just not' – he waved a hand ambiguously – '*for* women at all. I think most women of my acquaintance are glad of it.'

I grinned. '*I'm* glad of it.'

'Ah, and you are the one that counts.' His flush was furiously pink now. 'But you have, haven't you? Had interest in women. Before your marriage.'

'Yes,' I admitted. 'Before the army, and occasionally during my service. The women of the world are…' I sighed wistfully, teasing him a little. 'Well. You'd not appreciate it anyway.'

'And how are the *men* of the world?' Holmes asked curiously.

If he blushes any further, I thought smugly, *I shall have to take his temperature.* 'As diverse as the men of England.' I stood and leaned in to kiss those blushing cheeks. 'But I'm afraid I've forgotten them entirely,' I confided, smirking. 'Shall I show you why?'

'Oh, I imagine so,' Holmes murmured. 'But first – another brandy.'

Sherlock rose above me in the dark, his tall, thin form glowing in the bronzed light from the lamp. His chest heaved around his ribs, sweaty with exertion, and I reached up to steady him around his waist as he raised and lowered himself on my prick, inexorably, relentlessly captivating.

I shifted underneath him, squaring my hips and pressing myself up, chest to chest with him as he shuddered in my arms. He moved against me with abandon, and it was beautiful – it was *divine* – and I could not stop the words; I did not even know I was going to say them until I already had. 'Oh, God, Sherlock – *God*, I love you.'

There was a sharp inhale, and Sherlock stilled against me. I held my breath, staring up and waiting for him to respond, to return the sentiment – and suddenly I longed to hear it, *needed* to hear it. To know that it was true; to know that I was not here alone, utterly exposed.

He did not say it.

Instead he kissed me, hard, as though he could put the words back in my mouth, and began to move again, as though I had not said it at all. I closed my eyes, and felt something hot and sharp pull taut inside my chest and begin to break.

I found the article days later, tucked away in the back of the evening newspaper. It was barely three lines of text, but they filled me with dread: one of the Turkish bathhouses in Bishopsgate had been closed upon reports of immoral acts.

I knew the number listed for the place. I'd been there with Holmes.

I could scarcely breathe against the choking terror, but somehow managed to make an excuse to Mary before heading to Baker Street.

I had nearly sweat through my clothes by the time I arrived, and when I burst through the door, Holmes was on his feet in an instant to help me to a seat. 'Good Lord, John! Whatever is the matter?'

I brandished the paper, torn and crumpled from its journey in my nervous hands. It took him a moment to find the article, but when he did, the colour drained from his cheeks.

Finally he looked up. 'They don't keep accurate records,' he said, already reasoning his way through it. 'False names, and so on. They can't ever know that we were there.'

'Unless we were recognised.'

His hand found mine, stroking my skin. 'Did you ever recognise anyone there?' he asked gently.

'No,' I admitted, swallowing heavily. His touch had already begun to calm me. 'But still – perhaps we should avoid Bishopsgate.'

'Watson.'

I grunted. My leg hurt. My hands hurt too, actually – too cold, with a harsh sting along the knuckles. The voice came again, and this time I recognised it, and that hurt as well.

'Watson. Open your eyes.'

I did, lifting my chin from my chest with as good a glare as I could manage, which, in fairness, wasn't very good. The skin around my eye was hot and swollen. 'Holmes.'

'I see you've been down to the gambling clubs again,' Holmes huffed, reaching in to prod at a sore spot on my cheek. Bruise, probably. I hoped it would be brilliant. 'One of my street rats recognised you. You're lucky he came for me instead of the police. Can you walk? Where is your cane?'

'He broke it. With the back of his head,' I said, though I could not remember who exactly I meant.

'And how much did this gentleman take you for?' Holmes asked, entirely too perceptive.

I looked away. 'Everything I had on me,' I admitted quietly. 'And some I didn't.'

He sighed, lifting me to my feet and slinging an arm over his shoulder to carry me. 'Back to Baker Street then, I think. You can hardly go home like this.'

'Yes,' I agreed, stumbling along, sore and embarrassed. 'That may be for the best.'

It was raining again. The muted greys and violets of midnight washed over Sherlock's face, and I wondered if I'd ever see this peace in him in the light of day.

I stroked a finger over his cheek, hoping to rouse him just enough to say my goodnight. 'Sherlock,' I whispered. He shifted in the bed, mumbling something unintelligible; I leaned in to nudge my nose against his cheek. 'I have to go.'

Now his eyes slid open, confusion settling in their exhausted haze. 'Go?'

His gaze was so innocent in that moment, soft and mussed. It hurt me more deeply than I could say to realise that his sleep-worn mind had not considered that I might leave him. To know that he had forgotten our circumstances, and in dreaming had found some world where everything was different and we could share a bed all through the night.

'I can't fall asleep here,' I said gently. 'I have to go home.'

His brow furrowed again, then I saw understanding dawn sluggishly behind his eyes. 'Oh,' he said, blinking, 'of course.'

But he did not respond to my last kiss, and when I reached the door and looked back, he was curled under the blankets, holding a pillow to his chest as if to mimic the warmth and closeness of my body.

Chapter Fifteen

The case was an interesting one, and Holmes towered over it, a veritable tempest of whip-smart deductions and physical energy. He would have been intimidating on that score alone, but he also seemed to be agitated, tense and cold in his impatience; I tried not to let the sting of it distract me from the case.

As we left Scotland Yard, emerging into a wet, chilly night, I was already thinking of Baker Street and how we might find our common footing again, but I was surprised when Holmes stuck out his hand to shake mine. 'Goodnight,' he said, strangely formal.

I stared. 'Goodnight?'

He nodded. 'Yes, goodnight.'

'Holmes,' I said, with a nervous laugh. 'Let us get out of this rain and go back to Baker Street together.'

'There's no need,' he said, still with that polite tone. 'I understand you have obligations at home.'

Suddenly I understood – our delicate balance had been upset, and now he was attempting to put distance between us again. To remind himself of his place in my life as secondary, as a secret, as some private shame. 'Holmes,' I breathed, reaching out to stop him from this line of thought, but he had already stopped a cab for himself, and I could only stand there, struck dumb, watching as he left me behind.

I waited a week to go to him. The door to Baker Street barely opened before Holmes was crashing into me, fumbling the door's lock while he pressed eagerly against me. 'I'm sorry,' he said, crushing his mouth to mine, 'It was foolish to think – I don't know what – '

He was already down to his waistcoat, hair disheveled and feet bare; his kiss tasted like tea and alcohol, as if he had felt every sour, regretful feeling I had had over the last week and was pouring them back into me. I had come to try to be reasonable, to convince him in any way I could that I loved him, to do whatever I needed to in order to prove my contrition, but it seemed my argument had already been made for me, and accepted, and now forgiveness was the only thing left that I could give.

I could not deny him. I took his kisses and returned them twofold. 'I was the fool,' I managed before his hands flew to my trousers. He was going to have me against the door, and I was going to let him; I was helpless to do anything else under the gale force of his desperation. I arched into him, kissing my apology into his jaw, fingers flying to undo his buttons.

The fever took me quite by surprise; I was fine one night as I went to bed, and found the next morning that I could not summon the strength to get out of it again. On the third day of my illness, I surfaced long enough to ask that a message be sent to Holmes, informing him of my circumstance, but it must not have been sent straight away because it was already gone half-nine in the evening by the time I heard his voice carrying up the stairs, insisting upon seeing me.

Mary's voice cut in over his, not unkindly but very firm. 'He's in no fit state, Mr Holmes,' she said. I imagined them, stubbornness matched for stubbornness, and had to smile, though as I drifted I thought I had not heard such strength in her voice for some time.

I came to later when a warm compress was placed on my brow. Mary smiled down at me as she sat on the edge of the bed. 'Was Holmes here?' I asked.

'He was,' she confirmed. 'I told him he would have to come back tomorrow, if he wanted to see you. It was odd, you know – he can seem so aloof, but when I told him he couldn't see you, I thought he was going to beg.'

'Tell me something that no one else knows,' he said, slowing his movements, sucking at the hinge of my jaw as his hips rocked his cock gently inside me.

'Is now really the time?' I laughed, and he rewarded my cheek with a single deep thrust, driving the breath out of my lungs. I laughed again. 'I'm sure you know more about me than I know myself.'

Sherlock hummed against my neck; I could feel the vibration of it through my throat and into my chest. 'There are hundreds of things I don't know about you, John. Thousands.'

Suddenly, he no longer felt like he was with me – above me, yes, and inside me, but not *present*. As though between one thrust and the next, he had gone away, lost inside himself, and the rock of his hips and the drag of his cock had become automatic, painfully secondary to whatever thought he was having.

I clutched at him, digging my fingers hard into his neck. 'There's only one thing you need to know right now,' I said fiercely, startling him, watching as his eyes cleared again, 'and that's how it feels to have me on your cock, Sherlock Holmes. Now *fuck me*, and when we are finished I'll tell you absolutely anything in order to satisfy your great, bothersome brain.'

That brain was mercurial. With the arrival of never-ending rain the following weeks, Holmes took to his bed for days.

It wasn't physical illness, as far as I could tell. Just listlessness, a disinterested melancholy that he couldn't seem to shake off, not with articles from the papers – scientific or sensationalist – nor even with a puzzle or two from the odd client. Holmes had turned everyone away, barely even bothering to speak his dismissals aloud. Only I stayed. I would not go.

'I'm worried about you,' I whispered in the deepest moments of the night, having crept through the flat to lie beside him in the dark.

He looked at me across the pillows, bleary and overly warm from having been laid up in bed. He'd begun to smell a bit sour, as unwashed, unmoving bodies do when they've been lying in stuffy rooms for too long. He licked his lips, trying to smile.

'You must enjoy having your own use of the rooms.'

'You know I don't,' I chastised, finding Sherlock's hand in the sheets and holding it close. 'Come back to me soon, please.'

'I'm trying,' he answered, squeezing my hand. But then his eyes closed, and he was gone again, and I couldn't follow. I could only lie next to him, and wait for him to come back.

Chapter Sixteen

Baker Street was deserted at this hour of the night, and I was glad of it as I stumbled along the pavement. Any passersby would surely have thought me intoxicated or insane. I wished I was the former; I was not yet sure about the latter.

Holmes had dismissed me.

No, it was more than that, worse than that – he had cast me aside, thrown me over. He had risen from his chair, pale features set like unfeeling marble, and stated his decision to end our association without once looking at me, without explaining his reasoning. 'The reasons are immaterial,' he had said. 'The result is the same: we cannot continue. I would ask you to leave here, Watson. I would ask you not to return.'

I slumped against a wall and covered my face with my hands, thinking of the arguments I could've made, knowing that none of them would have made a difference. Holmes had refused to look at me. He had refused to hear that I loved him.

He had refused to say whether he had ever loved me.

'It is over,' he had said instead, turning away. 'It is done.'

I had never imagined I would hear him say such words. Now I thought I could feel them etch themselves, destructive and everlasting, into my very bones.

After that, the days ran together.

Mary must have known that something was deeply amiss. I told her it was only a bit of hay fever; a poor excuse, but at least it provided some explanation for my red-rimmed eyes and constant sniffling.

'Perhaps you should go and see Mr Holmes,' she suggested one evening, as she sat with her needlework and I stared into nothingness. 'Surely whatever falling out you had, it can be mended.'

She was always more perceptive than I gave her credit for. I laughed creakily, caught out in my lies as I was, and was grateful yet again for her unending kindness. I should have known better than to be untruthful to her. 'He asked me to never return,' I finally confessed. There didn't seem to be a reason not to be honest anymore. 'Our friendship, our partnership – it is done.'

Mary put aside her needlework and came to me; her hand in mine was so small, so soft. So unlike his. I clutched at her, pressed my lips to her skin.

'Let's go to the seaside,' she suggested gently, when I had gathered myself again. 'Or to the Continent. Somewhere out of London. It would do us some good, I think, to go somewhere you were not reminded of Mr Holmes, or of his business.'

I found the mention several lines deep in a newspaper article about a recent spate of killings out of Brixton. *Strangler Apprehended!* the headline blared. I had avoided all of the papers after we returned from the seaside, but before I could even reconsider it I was ducking into an alley to read one by weak lamplight, rewarded by the first mention of Holmes I had had in weeks.

Mr Sherlock Holmes, an amateur detective, the article read, *was of great assistance to Scotland Yard in their discovery of the Brixton Strangler.*

I read on, eager for more information, but that was the sum extent of Holmes' mention. The rest of the article detailed the Brixton Strangler's crimes and Detective Lestrade's ingenuity in investigation; I laughed to myself as I read, seeing Holmes' hand in every twist and turn the case had taken. He must have been brilliant, I thought. Just absolutely brilliant.

I stepped back out to the street, eager to head toward Baker Street, thinking of the congratulations I might offer him – but then I remembered suddenly I was not welcome there. I dropped the paper, startled at my own forgetfulness; I stared as the pages began to soak up the mud, and then took a deep breath and set off again toward home, trying to regain my bearings.

I looked up from my book, brow furrowed; across the sitting room, Mary coughed into a handkerchief.

'That's a nasty cough,' I commented. It sounded wet, as if it were deep in her lungs already. She'd had a cold the previous week, with cough and sore throat, but if the cough had lingered overlong, I hadn't noticed it until now. 'How long have you had it?'

She waved away my concerns. 'Only since last week, Doctor,' she said. 'I'm sure it'll be fine. You know London air sits a little heavily.'

Something in her manner seemed unusually flippant, though. I looked closer; she was too pale, I noticed, and probably too thin. 'You should tell me if you've been feeling poorly,' I said, putting my book aside and going over to feel her forehead. She wasn't unduly warm, but her skin was clammy; I wished I had my stethoscope handy to listen to her lungs and heartbeat.

'I didn't want to worry you,' she said. 'I know you've had quite a lot on your mind lately.'

'Even so,' I said. 'You must let me take care of you, Mary. I'll get a poultice for your chest tomorrow, and something to soothe your throat for now.'

She smiled wanly up at me. 'Something warm,' she agreed, 'and I think a little bland.'

It was past two in the morning when the knock came to our bedroom door, waking Mary and I with a start, and I knew immediately there was only one reason our housekeeper would have disturbed us. I put on my dressing gown and my hardest expression, and headed down into the parlour.

There he was: Sherlock Holmes.

He was *beautiful*.

'Watson,' he breathed, his eyes wide and surprised at the sight of me. 'I did not know if you would see me.'

I refused to grant him the same vulnerability. 'Holmes,' I said shortly. 'I have no idea what you could possibly want of me, but I assume it's important.'

Instantly, as though scalded by boiling water, he drew back. 'I apologise sincerely,' he said. 'It is a matter of urgency. I – there was no one else I could turn to.'

His manner was unusual, unnatural to him. I looked more closely; he was too thin, too haggard. 'It's a case?'

'Yes,' he said. 'I need your help, Watson. I cannot do this alone.'

As much as I wanted to turn him away, I couldn't deny him the opportunity to be heard. I gestured for him to take a seat, promising myself that I would keep my distance, steadfastly ignoring the way the very sight of him warmed my blood.

Though Holmes and I had spent several days in close quarters, on the run from Professor Moriarty's machinations, the tension and awkwardness did not seem any nearer to abatement. We barely knew how to talk to each other anymore.

'I should not have involved you,' Holmes said one night when we were in Brussels, delving his fingers into his hair in his frustration. 'You were well shot of me, and now I've dragged you in. It was an exceedingly poor decision on my part. I am sorry for it, old boy.'

My back stiffened at the endearment. I had not heard it in months, and though it was itself perfectly innocent, it still reminded me of warm nights in Baker Street, of seeking hands and seeking mouths, of secrets shared in moonlight. 'Perhaps you should stop making decisions on my behalf,' I said bitterly, remembering his decision to turn me from Baker Street.

Holmes looked up, his expression softening as he understood. 'That decision wasn't for you,' he admitted. 'It was the only decision I could make.'

'You sent me away,' I whispered. 'I thought maybe you had tired of me.'

'You were already gone,' he said, but slowly, as though he didn't know he were doing it, he reached out his hand.

I reached back. I would always reach back.

'It could be like this.'

Sherlock's head tilted back, his pale skin shining and damp with the efforts of our coming together, his dark hair stuck to his brow. He was ethereal and golden, pink with heat and warm with lassitude, and I pulled him closer, pressing a kiss to his shoulder. 'What could be like this?'

'We could,' he whispered. His voice was soft and dreamy; I thought he must be half-asleep already. 'The two of us. Traveling the world, staying one step ahead of our enemies. Conquering our own Napoleon, as it were. What do you think?'

I laughed. 'I think you get particularly fanciful after a good hard rogering.'

He turned onto his side, nudging his nose at mine. 'It'd be possible, you know,' he returned quietly. 'If you wanted.'

I blinked, suddenly concerned that he was taking the idea seriously, that he might actually be proposing that we make a run for it. 'You know we can't,' I said gently. 'Not really. There's Mary to consider, and your family – and never to return home? It would be no way to live, Sherlock.'

His eyes fluttered closed, hiding his thoughts. 'Of course,' he excused, 'just an idle daydream,' but his touch fell away, and his smile from across the pillows had gone small, and fragile, and brittle.

I waited for hours.

The roar of the falls dulled my ears; I could barely hear my own thoughts underneath the barrage of water, underneath the hiss of the spray and the chaos of my realisations.

The broken ferns and branches along the path told the story as well as if I had been here to see it myself: the confrontation, the struggle. Muddy footprints danced in the soil, glistening here and there as the drifting spray caught in the hollows. I touched my fingertips to them now and again, as if I could still feel Holmes' warmth in them. As if they could tell me whether he had thought of me, there at the end.

It could be like this, he had said. *The two of us. If you wanted.*

I had denied him and so he had sent me away, penned his goodbye as steadily as if he'd been at home at his desk, and followed Moriarty down into the cream and crack of the Reichenbach cauldron, clasped in the arms of his enemy.

I waited, calling out for him, praying that I might hear his voice call back to me, but the falls stole away the sound of my cries, and I was left with nothing but the half-human echo of the water breaking upon the rocks below.

CHAPTER SEVENTEEN

THE PAGE STRETCHED OUT IN FRONT OF ME, BLANK AND PRISTINE. I could think of a hundred stories I needed to tell, but I was not sure I could write down the ones I wanted to tell the most. Holmes' warnings rung in my ears as though he were in my study himself. *Things written down are always subject to discovery,* he whispered. *Perhaps you ought to make a mention of your wife.*

I didn't want to write about my wife.

I wanted to write about him. Not about Holmes – not about the great detective with the great mind. I wanted to write about *Sherlock.*

I wanted to write about his hands, his delicate fingers, his graceful movements. I wanted to write about the way he laughed, the way he flushed, the way he gasped under my touch. I wanted to write about his eagerness and his gentleness and his endless curiosity; I wanted to write about his eyes and his smile, his strength and his softness, and his love for me.

I didn't want to write accounts of his deductions and accomplishments. I wanted to create a portrait of the man, I thought, picking up my pen at last and putting it to the page. I wanted to draw him back into life and make the memory of him *breathe.*

'John.'

I looked up, blinking at the light of the lamp in Mary's hand; I hadn't noticed the fire burning out. 'What time is it?'

She put her hand to my forehead. 'He wouldn't have wanted to see you like this,' she said, her voice thick with sympathy. 'You must go up to bed, John. I've had the second bedroom made up for you.'

'The second bedroom?' We had slept separately before, but only when one of us was ill. I didn't think I was, but judging by the look on Mary's face, perhaps I was wrong.

'I thought you'd be more comfortable if you slept alone,' she said carefully. She twisted her hands, hesitating, as though she were trying to explain something she didn't quite understand herself. 'If you did not – if you did not mistake my warmth for his.'

I drew back, shocked. I should've denied the words, denied every one vehemently, but instead my eyes filled with tears and I could only bury my face in my hands. 'You knew. Mary. I'm so sorry.'

Her hands touched mine, stroking and soothing. 'I think I always have,' she said, as gently and kindly as I could never deserve. 'It's all right. You loved me as well as you could, John. But I've always known that you loved him better.'

That winter, Mary took a turn for the worse, and finally I realised the true depths of my depravity.

While I had been with Holmes, Mary had contracted tuberculosis. She was dying.

The infection worked quickly through her body, once it had begun. It made my veins run cold – that Mary had been suffering for months under my unseeing eye – but I could do nothing about it now. The helplessness ate at me the way the disease ate at her; at times I hoped it would prove just as fatal.

I thought about my mother, convalescing all those years alone by the sea, and of Mary's own holidays to the coast. I had thought she meant to escape my poor company for that of her friends; instead she had spent them in an attempt to prolong her life away from the prying eyes of her doctor husband, who had been too busy with his own affairs – literally and figuratively – to even notice.

In the end I had proved no better than my own father, than his hate and apathy.

My betrayal was as complete as any man's had ever been, and I could do nothing but watch as Mary wasted away, as her lungs began to disintegrate. I could do nothing but watch, as the pillows, drenched with sweat, turned bloody.

It didn't take long for the smell of Mary's sickroom to turn into that peculiarly sweet, rotting smell of a deathbed, and the long hours I spent next to her awoke memories of the base hospital at Peshawar.

I'd been sure I was going to die there. The enteric fever left me delirious, dehydrated, in terrible pain and in terrible weakness. With the lingering pain from the Jezail bullet on top of it, I had wanted to die.

Perhaps it'd been obvious. One of the nurses had taken a special interest in me, and when I asked her to tell me about the afterlife, she had instead insisted I be taken out to spend an afternoon on the verandah; my doctor had protested, sure it would kill me, but she'd stood firm: 'He's going to die anyway,' she had whispered, 'you may as well allow him some final sunshine.'

Once on the verandah, I had croaked to her, 'I heard you say that. You think I'm going to die.'

She had, surprisingly, smiled. 'Prove me wrong, and I'll apologise.'

Mary would not prove me wrong, no matter what sunshine I summoned. I could only wait, trying to remember that missionary's name, what she had looked like. Her hair had been dark, I thought, but her eyes – her eyes had been blue.

I slowly began to prepare for Mary's last days, and for the days that would come after. I nursed her, despite her protests – if I hadn't contracted the disease in Afghanistan, I told her, nor in the years living alongside her, I was unlikely to now – and tried not to think on whether it was better or worse to know the end was coming.

I didn't let her see my pain. For once in my damnable life, I tried to do what would make her happiest: reading to her, bringing new messages or gossip, recounting stories of India and Afghanistan, and even, once or twice and only ever at her own request, of Sherlock Holmes himself. This I could do; this I owed to Mary.

'Tell me what he was like,' she said, coughing. Fresh blood

sputtered onto the pillows, smearing red over the older rust of dried sputum. 'When you were together, the two of you.'

'You met him,' I reminded her, avoiding her true meaning. 'You knew him well, in fact.'

She shook her head, a rare smile playing on her lips. 'I didn't know him the way you did. No one did. Please, John. I want to be able to recognise him when I see him again.' She closed her eyes. 'I want to give him my blessing.'

In the end, I put away my journals. Packed up my pens and papers; gathered together all the half-completed thoughts stuffed into the various books and files and drawers of my writing desk. It was, in its own way, part of the ritual of mourning: as necessary and as clumsy and as heartwrenching as packing away Mary's dresses, as changing the sheets on her bed.

How does one accept a consolation graciously? How does one limit their responses to the polite *thank you* and the stiff upper lip? Mary's friends made their presentations in full etiquette, Mrs Cecil Forrester's eyes swimming in tears, reaching her gloved hands out to me, and I constantly felt two steps away from spilling out the truth: that I hadn't loved her as I ought to have. That I had loved her, but not well enough.

'You must tell us if there's anything we can do for you,' Mrs Forrester told me, as the fluttering ladies she'd arrived with dabbed at their eyes. I couldn't remember a single one of their names, and was left to watch them, wondering whether they were here out of honest grief or just in observance of the procedure. 'We're so terribly sorry.'

'Thank you,' I said, instead of saying what I meant: *not as sorry as I will always be.*

As the weeks passed, I was surprised at how many people seemed to hear of Mary's death and think immediately of Sherlock Holmes, as if the world saw their passing as two sides of the same event.

My editor had begged me to write a novel of the events of

Holmes' death – 'For the public's mourning, Watson! How could you deny them?' – but I'd emphatically declined. The public didn't need to know the details of Holmes' death in order to mourn him; they only wanted the details for the salaciousness of it, to imagine his expression as he went over the Reichenbach Falls, to prod at the depths of my grief. They didn't want to mourn Sherlock Holmes; they wanted to mourn a hero.

I did not know that hero, and no story about Holmes' death would have included the story of Mary's. I could never tell one without the other's, I knew, and so I could not tell either at all.

I packed up the house Mary and I had shared and moved into smaller quarters on Queen Anne Street. I took more patients and worked longer hours. A year passed, then two, and finally the public began to forget about Holmes.

For myself, I remembered, and even after I came out of the mourning suits, I remained in black.

So it went, for years. I walked. There wasn't anything else to do.

The chill of London pressed in on me, suffocating me under the never-ending rains that threatened to wash the city out. The cold ran down into my bones; my feet, constantly damp, grew raw and red with sores. I walked and walked, going nowhere, trying to escape the fate I'd brought upon myself: a cold and hollow existence, bereft of those I'd loved.

I had betrayed them, Sherlock and Mary. Selfishness and cowardice had guided my hands, and now they both lay dead at my feet as surely as if I had dealt the final blows myself. No amount of contrition was going to bring them back from where they'd drowned in the depths of my neglect – in the waters of the Reichenbach, in the blood of her own lungs.

The lamps were no match for the wretched days and nights, and the shadows grew long under the rain. I walked Oxford Street, then Hampstead Road, then set into Regent's Park. Even those walkways were vacant, and I walked them slowly, remembering the days I'd wandered them arm-in-arm with a lover.

When next I remembered myself, I was standing before Baker Street. I looked up, but all the lights were out, and the windows were empty and black.

'That's never Doctor Watson? Why, hello!'

I turned, and there on the pavement was none other than Inspector Lestrade of Scotland Yard, hurrying toward me, half-grimacing, half-smiling. It had been more than two years since I'd seen him.

'Oh, Inspector!' I greeted.

Lestrade took my hand, obviously in earnest. 'The good Doctor,' he said. 'There is not a day that goes by that *his* name is not thought among those at Scotland Yard, you know.'

There was a sharp pain in my chest. 'Is that – is that so?' I asked faintly. *His* name. As though his was the only name.

'I tell all the new constables,' Lestrade went on, oblivious, not letting go of my hand. 'I worked with him! I had the chance to observe the genius at his work, to see the bloodhound in his element. Sherlock Holmes! We are very proud of him down at Scotland Yard, yes, we are, and of you as well.'

'Oh, erm, thank you,' I managed, taken quite aback. 'He was the genius, though. I only took the notes.'

'We have thought of you since his passing,' Lestrade said, still ignoring me. 'You have our condolences, sir. He was a very great man, and you must be missing his friendship, sir. We, too, are missing more of him than just his amazing brain.'

My chance meeting with Lestrade opened a wound in me, and it was one that could not be staunched.

Memories of Holmes, which I'd firmly repressed over the last few years, blossomed again in my mind. The quirk of his grin, the light of his eyes, the warmth of his hands – the details of all our adventures came rushing back, prodding at the loneliness I'd become so accustomed to. I remembered the rush of our feet against the cobblestones, the gas lamps piercing the fog, the adrenalin of his quick strength and his confident conclusions.

My journals had sat in dust too long. I brushed off the neglect and opened them, remembering the dreamlike haze in which I'd written those last words, the detached reality in which I'd lived before Mary's condition had finally come to my horrifyingly belated attention.

Could I really revisit all of those words now?

Could I finally tell Sherlock Holmes' last story?

Could I revisit the Reichenbach Falls, the swirling mist of that devilish cauldron that had claimed him? Could I revisit the hours I had spent, tracing his footsteps in the damp paths, wondering what his last thoughts had been?

I didn't know if this would finally close Sherlock Holmes' wound in my heart, but I picked up my pen, and, once more, I began.

I was still awake when the night began to lighten. I put down my pen, watching from my bedroom window as deep violet turned to grey, as pink brushed along the horizon. Once I might've thought it beautiful, a display of hope and survival – a sign that I had lasted out the night. Now it only heralded another day to spend going through the usual mechanisms – having breakfast, seeing patients, picking at dinner – as I waited for the sanctuary of the dark.

The lone solace I granted myself was in the newspapers and my journals, in accounts of the many crimes and intrigues that plagued the public. I scoured each article, using the methods I had learned at the hand of the world's foremost criminal expert, but more often than not I found myself distracted from the evidence and arguments by the ghost that walked between the lines.

Sometimes I could even see him again: his tall, lean figure stalking around a room, flourishing his hands, pointing out this clue or that. I wondered what clues he might see about me now, what deductions he might make. Whether I would catch his eye the way I had that first night together, so many years ago.

Whether Sherlock Holmes would still want to deduce the fragments that were left of his Boswell.

There are a thousand ghosts in London.

I could still see Sherlock Holmes sometimes, in this restaurant or that news-agent's. I saw him sitting at the table in Simpson's where I'd first fallen in love with him; I could see him in Regent's Park, turning his sharp gaze to the spring leaves. His face peered out of passing cabs and shop windows. He stood with Mary behind the columns of the Lyceum Theatre, turning their faces toward me, expecting me to follow along.

In the spring of 1894, London gained a new ghost: the Honourable Ronald Adair, the murdered young man that became the subject of great interest in what was known as the Park Lane Mystery.

I'd been trying to resolve the mystery as a little exercise of Holmes' old methods, but hadn't gotten very far; I thought perhaps viewing the scene would be instructive. If Inspectors Lestrade or Gregson were in charge, I might stand some chance of being invited in. I set out, but it was no good; I did not recognise any of the constables.

It didn't matter, I thought, as I helped gather the books I had knocked out of some old bibliophile's arms. There were many ghosts in London, but none of them were real, and no ghost of Sherlock would fill his place besides.

I didn't understand. I *couldn't* understand.

The remnants of the old, decrepit bookseller sat discarded on my examination table; a spectre sat in my patient's chair. I heard his voice, smelled the smoke of his cigarette, and still I barely dared believe it.

'I owe you a thousand apologies,' Sherlock Holmes had said, offering a smile. 'I had no idea you would be so affected.'

He was alive. Sherlock was *alive*, and joyful, sitting in my chair and telling me stories of Tibet and France and everywhere in between, of exploring everything and learning anything and gathering what information he could about Professor Moriarty.

He'd watched me, that night at the Reichenbach Falls. He'd

watched as I cried out for him. As I believed that he had gone willingly into the water. As I believed that, in denying him the whole of my life, I had driven him to his death.

Every word he spoke cut me deeply, but I couldn't turn away from him for fear that he would disappear again. Instead I put on a trembling smile to match his own, locking away my despair. No idea, he'd said, that I would be so affected, and I decided, then and there, that if Holmes could not deduce it, I would never show him the true extent of my bereavement.

Chapter Eighteen

I had been consumed by a fantasy — or else by a nightmare. I was not yet sure.

Holmes flitted around his old rooms at Baker Street as though he'd never left them, examining his books, and expounding on his deductions. It was as though he'd already forgotten his time abroad, and now intended to take up his old post as though nothing had changed.

Everything had changed.

I had changed.

My mask of delight and relief finally began to falter. I wanted nothing more than to go home, to bury my face in my hands and burn out every pointless thought I'd had, blaming myself for things that had not even happened. Despising myself for things that weren't even true.

Holmes, incredibly, mistook my troubled mind for exhaustion. 'Why don't you lie back on the sofa,' he said, putting his books aside, 'and take some rest, dear boy.'

He reached out, as though to guide me back, but I recoiled from his touch, and the first hint of distress appeared in his features. 'You're safe here,' he said, his voice gone soft and soothing. 'I understand it's quite the shock.'

I laughed, helplessly, but I could not relax in that eerily familiar room with my eerily familiar companion. In the end, I took the first opportunity I could find, and bolted.

I felt like my chest was being ripped open as I ran. Like my fragile heart was finally being torn in two.

I'd been naught but a pawn in Sherlock's game, and I'd been

played – a worthy actor on the stage for the benefit of Moriarty's actors, and then even as the need for deception had passed, I'd been forgotten. All the pain and grief and mourning I had suffered, every sleepless night, every nightmare, every moment trying to close the wound in my chest that Holmes had left behind: simply, utterly meaningless.

He was alive.

He was alive, and I'd barely survived the years of his silence and his duplicity. He was alive, traveling the world, conducting experiments, learning and exploring, and I had been in London, watching as Mary slipped away, clinging to my own survival.

I raged through my rooms for days, swearing never to see him again, but when I finally picked up my papers, my half-written accounts of our adventures, drawing back my hand to throw them into the fire, I could not make myself do it.

In life or in death or in resurrection, no matter how heartsick or heartbroken, would I always be drawn toward Sherlock Holmes? Would I never really be free of him?

Would the ties between us never truly be broken?

I went back. Of course I did.

There was a figure in the window at Baker Street.

At first I thought it was another of Holmes' bust tricks, but after a moment, it lifted a violin to its shoulder and set a bow against the strings. I wished I could hear what he was playing, but there was only the silence of the last three years.

I hadn't seen him since his resurrection, six weeks ago; I'd ignored his telegrams, declined his invitations. Yet I knew he would play for me if I asked. He would play until I slept, and then wake me with his hand on mine, or perhaps my cheek, with a soft smile and a suggestion in his eyes.

It frightened me, how much I wanted that. There had been so many lies, so many years, and still I wanted that. I wished I could have felt only what I ought to have in the wake of his many betrayals, but Holmes was *alive*, playing me a song from the first floor window, and that was more than any man before me had dared to dream of.

I wasn't sure about anything else, but our friendship, at least – yes. I could offer that.

I squared my shoulders and stepped forward, reaching for the last of my bravery.

He apologised, of course.

Perhaps he could see the strain his resurrection had had on me – I could certainly see it in the mirror myself. I'd lost weight over the last six weeks; I'd slept little and eaten less. I hardly meant to showcase my grief, but Holmes always had been able to see through me; I did not appreciate the reminder.

But he did apologise, and he didn't attempt to offer excuses. 'I'm sorry,' he had said plainly. 'I am so sorry to have caused you pain, John.'

As if he hadn't expected me to have suffered. As if he hadn't expected me to blame myself.

I had asked him once, long ago, how he would have felt if I'd risked my life, and then he said he would have understood – if it were for the case. It had felt like a dismissal then; I understood now that it had been a warning.

But he apologised, and I could not help myself. I didn't want to. I accepted.

'I have my own life now,' I said, a bit coldly. 'So our acquaintanceship can be renewed, but I'm afraid I have time for little else.'

'Of course,' Holmes agreed quickly. I looked away, avoiding his eyes as he lowered them with gratitude, as his cheeks turned red with an embarrassed blush.

I ought to have known that Holmes would begin taking clients again as soon as he was able, but I was still surprised when I arrived at Baker Street one evening days later to find him in consultation with an elderly gentleman wearing a clerical collar.

'My apologies,' I said to them both, ducking back. 'Holmes, I shall wait downstairs.'

'If you wouldn't mind, actually,' he said quickly, jumping up to stop me before I could close the door, 'I could use your assistance, Doctor Watson.'

An irrational anxiety flooded through me: the last case I'd been on with Holmes had ended with his death. I hesitated, but the client was waiting, so all I said was, 'I'm afraid I'm quite unable. The work no longer suits me.'

Holmes squinted in confusion, reading what I would not say; I allowed it, and soon a terrible understanding dawned in his eyes. 'Oh,' he said. 'Oh, I see.'

Regret flashed hotly over the apprehension in my stomach. He hid his remorse and shame over his deception quite well, but I knew him better than he remembered, and could see what others would not. 'Well, perhaps I could stay and hear the gentleman's story,' I offered finally. 'Just the story, mind.'

He hurried to agree. 'Of course,' he said, but he was smiling brilliantly.

There were arms. The length and strength of arms, the smell of tobacco smoke, a breath falling upon my ear. I could almost hear the voice in it, leaning in, straining in, and suddenly I was straining against, straining *with*, rocking into his heat –

I woke with a start. There were tears in my eyes.

I rolled over, burying my face in the pillows and willing my prick to soften. I refused to frig myself to the memories of a body I thought I'd never touch again – a body that was now within my reach, if only I dared to hold out my hand.

I saw it in Holmes, sometimes: the heat that had once burned so easily between us. I saw aborted movements towards me, his hands closing around themselves as though he longed for something warm to fill their emptiness. I did not remember him having been so obvious.

Part of me wanted desperately to give in, to breathe my relief into his skin and feel the life in him with all the life in me – but whenever I saw that desire in his eyes, I remembered how it felt to wake up without him, that morning after the terrible falls.

It was better to restrain myself, I thought, than to give him another chance to leave me behind.

I hardened myself with caution; I felt I had to.

'It would be the most logical arrangement,' Holmes said, coming to the end of his speech. 'As well as the most economical.'

He was carefully nonchalant, but he apparently hadn't realised that his caution gave him away. It wasn't the first time over the last year he'd hinted at wanting me to move back, but his insistence was draining us both. I gave the same response I'd given before. 'I cannot abandon my practice.'

There was a long silence, then he threw down his instruments with a clatter. 'You mean you can't abandon your penitency,' he said bitterly.

I was shocked at his vehemence. 'Perhaps some penance would do you good,' I returned, defensive and insulted. 'For myself, I can't so easily forget my grief.'

'It's not grief,' Holmes snapped. 'It's nothing but guilt and punishment for my death, which you did not cause, and Mary's, which you couldn't have prevented, and I'd see you free from the pain of it.'

I got to my feet, my face hot and hands shaking. 'You know nothing of the pain I've felt,' I said, quiet and fierce. 'You've relinquished your say in what I do and how I feel. There are limits now, Holmes. I will not allow you to cross those boundaries.'

As a dozen times before, I should have stayed away from Baker Street after that. I should've avoided Holmes and his awkward company, his mournful eyes, his attempts to give me a reason to come more often, to stay into the evenings. I should've immersed myself once more in my practice, or perhaps in the writing of a medical treatise, or even joined a new club, but I did not.

Instead I accepted his every invitation, and made some of my own, even though our interactions remained strange and stilted. I took him to restaurants that had sprung up in the years he'd been gone, where we'd eat in silence; he took me to concerts and ballets where we said not a word beyond *hello* to one another all evening. I went to Baker Street and picked newspapers off his desk to read; he sent me gifts of pipe tobacco and books and never included a note.

I resented it, this weakness in me. The discomfort in my belly that grew and grew when I'd not seen him for several days, when I'd not heard from him. I resented it, but I did not stop myself.

I was desperate to be near Holmes, and I only hoped that these little tastes of him would be enough to continue holding me back.

The next evening had an uneasy, sour feeling to it; the spaces between us seemed as wide as they had ever been. Several times I thought to leave, but could not make myself. Uneasy silences between Holmes and I still seemed better than the empty silences of a night alone.

Finally, it seemed, Holmes could take the unrest no longer. He cleared his throat. 'I thought I ought to say,' he said, still staring, unseeing, at his papers. 'I did not hear of Mary's death until I had landed back in London. That you were alone, all that time – I didn't know. I was so sorry to hear it.'

There was a long, awful pause as I understood his meaning: that he didn't know he would condemn me to years of solitude. That he had thought, in leaving, that he was freeing me from the misery of my divided heart. 'Would it have made a difference, had you known?'

He still couldn't look up at me. 'Yes,' he admitted softly. 'I was trying to spare you, John. I did not mean to leave you to face your grief alone.'

I nodded, straining against the sudden knot in my throat. 'Thank you,' I managed, and though the rest of the night passed in silence, a new understanding between us began to blossom.

His violin spoke in the silence when we could not. It was soft at first, so soft I barely noticed it begin. Holmes stayed in the shadows, just beyond the reach of the flickering light of the fire as though to hide himself. The music gentled over us both, easing the night into the room; something hot and fluttering settled beneath my breast, seeing him so familiar and foreign at once. He swayed with the music the way he had hundreds of times before, but he played a tune I didn't know.

I missed him still, I realised. Only feet away, and I missed him desperately, and suddenly I understood that I was in danger of losing something precious if I did not act.

I took a deep breath. 'I've missed hearing you play.'

Holmes turned to look at me, surprise in his eyes, but slowly, tentatively, the song began to shift and slow, resetting into something sweetly, terribly familiar, like something from long ago, something I'd forgotten in a dream. *I have missed playing for you,* the melody said.

Our eyes met, and I saw what neither of us had dared to say: *I have missed you.*

It was suddenly too much; I looked away, ashamed but unable to stop myself. I wasn't yet ready to lay myself so bare.

'It's just a scratch,' Holmes repeated to himself, once we were back at Baker Street and I was settled into my chair. I had appropriated a shawl from Nathan Garrideb's curious rooms to protect my modesty where Holmes had cut up my trousers, but now he untied the makeshift covering and laid bare the minor injury to my thigh.

Holmes slowly got to his knees before me, where he cleaned the wound carefully, examining it at every angle; his touch was almost clinical, as brief and steady as my own hands had been against many such wounds.

If it weren't for my own hands – capable as they were, and by far the more suited to the cleaning and dressing of a scratch – I might have thought Holmes was merely seeing to me out of professional interest. As it was, though, he could not seem to stop repeating himself, *it's just a scratch*, and his eyes were rimmed with pink.

I let him apply the bandage, wondering when last I had seen such a look of naked affection for me on another's face – if I had ever seen such a look on his. I couldn't remember, and it seemed suddenly like the failing was mine, not Holmes', and I thought that maybe I simply hadn't known how to look at him before.

He took to watching me, as he was now, standing in firelight, elbow propped on the mantel.

My breath caught when I finally noticed. I'd never before seen such a look on Holmes, one of longing and hopelessness, as though my very presence pained him but he could not look away.

I wanted to go to him. I wanted to take his face in my hands and smooth away those lines. I wanted to kiss his mouth – taste the lingering smoke of his pipe, feel for myself his warmth, his breath. I went so far as to grip the arms of my chair, ready to lift myself, when I remembered that I could not do any of these things by my own edicts.

I couldn't now remember why I had made them.

'Can you ever forgive me?' he asked softly. 'Can you ever truly forgive me the grief I caused you, Watson? Can you ever see past that horrible act and see me, as a man, standing before you?'

I felt this was the most important question Holmes had ever asked me. 'What would happen if I did?' I asked in return. 'What would happen if I did not?'

He looked back into the fire. 'I will never ask you again,' he finally said. 'I cannot heal what has been broken.'

Very slowly, I stood. 'No,' I said. 'You cannot. You've not lived with the loss I have, Holmes. It hardly matters to me that you stand here tonight alive, because I'm still reliving the horror of realising your loss every day, even as you breathe before me. No amount of revelations and resurrections is ever going to take away the day I lost you.'

Holmes' head lowered; he did not look to me. 'I didn't understand what I was doing,' he said finally. 'I am sure I still don't understand what I've done. I can only say that I'm so sorry for having done it. I didn't understand your heart as clearly as I thought I did.'

'I know,' I answered. 'I forgive you anyway.'

His head jerked up; his eyes on me were wide, disbelieving. 'You – ? But why?'

I took another step toward him. His hand, when I reached for it, was warm from the fire; the palm was sweating. 'I forgive you anyway,' I repeated, 'because it is causing me more pain to withhold it. I forgive you because it is causing you pain, and I can't bear it. I forgive you because I can do nothing else, Sherlock Holmes. Yes, I so very much forgive you.'

'Watson,' he said, 'John,' and I finally stopped holding myself back.

The kiss was barely more than a tremble, barely more than a thought and a breath, a brush of lip to uncertain lip. I waited, heart hammering around the sort of preternatural calm I could only ever remember feeling on the battlefield, the sort of eager patience that comes with readiness, with anticipation. I waited, feeling Holmes' every shivery breath against my cheek.

'John,' he said finally, 'I confess I did not know you were going to do that.'

I drank in the sight of him, and could not stop myself from breathing out a laugh. 'Neither did I.'

The tentative smile on his mouth began to fade, and his eyes slid away. 'Did you mean it?' he asked, full of caution.

I cupped his face with my hands. 'When you first came back, I never wanted to see you again,' I told him. 'But we two are bound, Sherlock Holmes. Permanently.' My thumbs smoothed over his cheeks. 'Yes, I meant it.'

I had not kissed him in more than three years. I leaned in again, promising myself that it would be worth the risk, worth any risk – worth prosecution or prison or even abandonment again – to have him now. I would kiss him as long as he would let me, and pay whatever price it cost to save our bond.

His body was long and lean underneath mine, and I lost myself in him for a while, exploring every inch as though it were new ground.

Sometimes, in fact, it was.

There were scars on him I didn't recognise, evidence of injuries he had suffered that I hadn't been there to grumble over and to mend, scattered about his flesh like silvery-pink constellations. It was undeniable proof that his adventures over the last three years had sometimes veered away from fantastical and into treacherous, and I kissed every last wound, closing my eyes, wishing I could have spared him every one, wishing I could have borne the pain for him. 'I lost you,' I murmured into his damaged skin.

Sherlock cupped the back of my head and held me close. 'I'm here,' he assured me. 'I'm alive, John. I came back.'

I slipped up his body, finding his mouth with mine. 'Did you ever wonder if you might not?'

'Sometimes,' he admitted. 'It was a rough-and-tumble time, John.'

'Promise you'll never do it again.' I kissed his cheeks, his eyelids, begging without words.

'I don't want to ever do it again, not without you,' he answered, and that was good enough for me. I lowered myself against him, pressing into him, until the lines between our two bodies began to blur.

'You don't think I'm attached to you, do you?' Sherlock's voice was quiet in the dark. 'You think you're – what? Convenient?' I didn't answer. He was perfectly capable of deducing what I would say anyway, and I was naked enough already. 'You're not at all convenient, John Watson. Nothing about you is convenient.'

I cleared my throat, wet my dry lips. 'It's not important.'

'It's the most important thing in the world,' he said, almost irritably, 'because I am in love with you. I've always been in love with you, and you don't know it.'

I blinked up at his bedroom ceiling, letting the words sink down into me. 'Oh,' I said finally. 'You never said.'

He huffed, rolling to hide his face in my shoulder. *Shy*, I thought, marveling at the idea. *Afraid, underneath all that bravado, and of me.* 'I suppose I thought I was protecting myself.'

I turned to face him, coaxing his eyes up. I could see now so many of the same uncertainties that had plagued me, the doubt and the disbelief. 'Sherlock,' I breathed, touching my forehead to his, 'I will vow to you now: you will never need protection from me.'

I kissed him, and he sobbed a laugh against my mouth and he kissed me back, free and beautiful and absolutely, wondrously breathtaking.

It was late by the time Holmes came home – late enough to almost be considered early. I was still sitting up, looking through some old case notes and waiting for him; he was clearly trying to be quiet enough to sneak by my room. A handkerchief was pressed to his forehead. 'Ah, Watson,' he said when he saw me. 'You're awake.'

'Yes,' I said, getting to my feet. 'Are you all right?'

'Oh, yes,' he answered, eying his handkerchief guiltily. I went to him, and eventually managed to get my hand around his elbow and guide him to a chair. 'This is nothing.'

'Then you won't mind my having a look,' I reasoned, but he would not remove his handkerchief. 'Sherlock. I can obviously see that you've injured yourself. I'm a doctor, after all. You must be concussed as well, to think me so easily fooled.'

Chagrined, he finally withdrew his hand. There was indeed a gash upon his forehead, still bleeding quite freely. 'You thought you'd hide this from me?' I asked incredulously.

'I thought it might distress you,' he admitted. 'I wanted to spare you, if I could.'

'I should think myself much more distressed at being lied to,' I chided softly, kissing his uninjured temple to reassure him, and he apologised softly as I reached for a bandage.

We ran.

It was like it had always been. London seemed to carry us as we flew down her streets and alleys after our quarry. If Holmes was right – and I trusted he was – the scoundrel would lead us right into the heart of one of the most secretive societies in Britain, like a spider leading us into the nest.

It didn't really matter, I thought, my heart bursting and skin thrumming with adrenalin. I was step in step with Sherlock beside me, our feet striking one rhythm on the pavement, and I'd run forever next to him. I would run wherever he might lead me.

Our suspect veered into an alley, and Holmes pulled me against the wall so he could peer around the corner. 'All right, Watson?'

I meant to say, *yes, what's happening?* Instead what I said, surprising us both, was, 'I love you.'

Holmes looked back at me, incredulous. 'Is this really the time?' he asked. 'We're about to catch a murderous sect of monks.'

'Needs must,' I shrugged, utterly unembarrassed.

He cast a quick glance around to make sure we were alone, then kissed me, hard, right there in the open street. 'I love you, too,' he said, laughing, though his eyes were serious. 'Now that that's settled – I think it's time to stop this blasphemy.'

My joys continued to multiply.

'Here, now,' Holmes said, stopping me right outside the sitting room with a hand on my chest and a smile on his lips. 'Close your eyes.'

I obliged him, laughing in response to his good mood. He opened the door and left me standing in the hall, and then I could hear the soft strains of music. At first I thought he'd picked up his violin, but then a hand took mine, startling me, and he pulled me toward the centre of the room.

'All right,' he said, near my ear. A hand settled on my hip; the other shifted in my hand, moving into position for a dance. 'Open your eyes.'

I did, grinning wide. 'You've acquired a gramophone.'

'You enjoy my music,' he said, with an almost bashful smile. I was transfixed by it. 'And the concert halls. And I wanted very much to ask you to dance.'

'Then I shall do my best,' I promised, squeezing his hand, 'though I warn you, I'm not very good.'

Together we fell into a rhythm, moving around the sitting room step by step. I was clumsy compared to his elegant bearing, but he didn't seem to mind.

'You'll pick it up in no time,' he assured me, laughing again. 'There, see – you've already found the beat.'

CHAPTER NINETEEN

THE GENTLE RHYTHM OF THE TRAIN WAS A COMFORTING, SOOTHING movement beneath us as we made our way back toward London. The case had led us out to a farm in Somerset, where, after three grueling days, Holmes had finally discovered the murderer hiding away in the root cellar of his dilapidated family home.

With the culprit in irons, we'd caught the last train out of Taunton. Holmes had begun the journey with a sly grin and a conspiratorial eye, but I knew he was exhausted beyond his limitations, and in the privacy of our compartment, I had only kissed him briefly, and then held him as he succumbed to the physical demands of his body.

He did not often push himself like this anymore, and I was grateful there seemed to be some reprieve in sight for his later years. When we first had lived together, I'd often feared that he would sacrifice his health and, ultimately, his life in pursuit of his work. Now, I thought, with a grateful smile, he had other pursuits to occupy his thoughts.

The sky was beginning to brighten as we approached the bustle of the city. I kissed Sherlock's brow, waking him gently. 'Nearly there,' I murmured, watching him sniff in protest. 'Time to go home and get you to a proper bed.'

'Hullo! What's this?' Holmes said, picking up a copy of *The Strand* from our sideboard. '"The Sussex Vampire." Tell me, Watson, did you manage to admit your usefulness in filing *Vampirism in Hungary*, so long ago?'

'Mm.' I had been drowsing on the sofa for a few hours, occasionally waking to a kiss or to Holmes' rambling speech. He was especially spirited tonight, but his busyness only served as a comfortable reminder that he was there, and I smiled up at him. 'I don't believe I made mention of myself, no.'

'You never make mention of yourself if you can help it,' he said, flipping open the magazine. He read the story aloud, his voice brimming with pride and fascination.

'It was a good case,' I said, on its conclusion. 'You're right to be proud of it.'

'My dear boy,' he laughed. 'It's not the case I am proud of, but you. The successful writer, who has made so much of me.'

'I thought you didn't like my stories,' I protested, without heat. 'Over-romantic simplifications, are they not?'

He leaned over the sofa, kissing me in order to quiet me. 'I'm allowed to change my opinion.'

The kissing lasted a while longer, but I grumbled obligingly when he pulled away, making sure not to laugh. 'Your opinion, dearest, is awfully biased.'

Sherlock stretched beneath me, sighing deeply as he shivered through the aftershocks of his orgasm. I am sometimes biased too, for I loved him like this, loose and relaxed, still trembling with the force of my effect on him. I kissed his cheek and jaw until he laughed and pushed me playfully away.

'Hush now,' he said, closing his eyes with a smile. 'I want to sleep next to you for a while before I have to go back to my own bed.'

'You can sleep late,' I told him, dodging his hands and sliding in to press a kiss to his ribs and his belly, just barely beginning to go soft with age. He was still sticky with our combined fluids, though I'd cleaned most of it away. 'You do half the time anyway.'

'Mrs Hudson must think we are the laziest tenants in all London,' he agreed, giggling again as he tried to escape my ticklish kisses. 'Haven't you had enough?'

'No,' I said, laughing against him. 'I'll never have enough of you.'

'Yes, well,' he said. I knew without looking that he would be blushing; I looked anyway. 'You're incorrigible.'

I could not deny it. 'I can hardly be blamed,' I said, sliding up to kiss him properly, smiling against his mouth. 'It's your fault for being beautiful.'

'Holmes, wait.' I caught at his arm before he could take off, eager to find a hansom before the suspect got away. 'I'll meet you at home when this is done.'

Holmes met my eyes with surprise and concern. 'You're not coming?'

I tapped my cane against the pavement. 'I think an able-bodied man would be better suited for the task tonight,' I said. 'Take Hopkins instead, and do try to avoid trouble.'

If we'd been alone, Holmes would almost certainly have reached to massage my thigh, offering to soothe the old wound with tender hands. Instead he clasped his own hands together as if to stop himself. 'You're very certain?'

'Entirely. Finish this up and then come tell me the entire story. I'll want to take notes for *The Strand,* you realise, so be sure to remember the details just right.'

Holmes grinned. 'So you can disregard them in due time?'

'I must disregard them upon my own judgement,' I explained, in a haughty tone. 'Which means I must have all of them to begin with, so I can pick them off at my leisure.'

'I could see you home, at least. The theft has already occurred – it would not prejudice the case if I – '

'*Go*,' I laughed, cutting him off. 'Just be sure to catch the damn blackguard.'

I was already in bed by the time Holmes arrived back to Baker Street. I heard him come in and set a few things on the table, and had barely managed to raise myself to my elbows when the door opened and he came in, illuminated by the dark light of a lamp.

'Oh,' he whispered, startled. 'You're here.'

'Hope you don't mind,' I whispered. 'My leg, and the stairs – '

'Not at all, old boy.' He set down the lamp, stripping off his

117

collar and waistcoat. 'Is it any better? Anything I could do?'

I eased myself back against the pillow. 'No,' I sighed. 'Just wait for it to pass. Mary used to – ' I cut myself off. I didn't speak of Mary if I could help it, and especially not here, in Sherlock's bed, just as he was about to join me. Every thought of her was a swell of guilt over my heart; every mention of her was a stab of hurt into Sherlock's.

'It's – ' he hesitated, cleared his throat. He was standing next to the bed in nightshirt and bare feet, as though he couldn't bring himself to get in. 'It's all right. Tell me.'

'I don't even remember what I was going to say,' I lied, but Holmes shook his head, and called my bluff.

'You do,' he said. 'But you don't wish to say. I don't mind, John. I know you must think of her sometimes. I know you must miss her as you missed me.'

I wished he would put out the lamp so I would not have to see his face as he said such a thing. 'I don't care to make you uncomfortable,' I said. 'Let's forget it. Come to bed.'

He did, but after I was sufficiently pillowed against him, his long fingers rubbing into the sore muscles of my leg, he spoke again, very quietly. 'I would not have you pretend that she wasn't a part of your life, you know. It would hardly be fair to you, and hardly fair to her.'

'But is it fair to *you*?' I returned. 'To be reminded of such heartache as I caused us?'

'Isn't it? To know your heart to be capable of such love?' His fingers on my chin tilted my face up. 'I would have her remembered, not forgotten.'

I had not been aware of the pressure on my chest, but it eased so suddenly I was moved almost to tears; I kissed him, trying to explain what I could not say. 'Thank you.'

'You're a good man, John Watson,' he said. 'And Mary will live well beyond her burial.'

It was a quiet evening, and I was making the most of it, writing furiously as Holmes plucked an absent tune on the violin. The story had taken hold of me and I was reaching the climatic deduction, speeding along as fast as the ink would allow, words coming easily, dialogue flowing naturally, and –

And Holmes made an ugly noise across the violin strings. I startled in my chair. 'Sherlock Holmes!' I looked back at the page, but the words seemed far away now. 'I've lost my focus.'

Holmes put the violin aside. 'However can I make it up to you?'

Clearly, he'd grown jealous of the attention I was placing in his fictitious counterpart. I sniffed, unaffected by the display. 'By leaving me alone and sitting very quietly for the next hour.'

'Oh, come now,' he said. 'Surely it can't be that difficult to regain your focus?'

'It *is*,' I said. 'You know very well you don't like interruptions when *you're* working.'

'Yes, but *I* do finely detailed chemical work.'

'Finely detailed! You don't know the half of it, my dear fellow. You try writing one down, if you're so sure of yourself.'

'Fine,' he answered, 'I shall,' and he came to steal away my pen. I let him, sitting back and waiting for his show of confidence to backfire.

I did not wait long.

'Here now, Watson,' Holmes said, putting a gleeful full stop on the page he'd just finished. 'Not only have I proven anyone can write a little story, I've thought up a brilliant solution to our little problem, and you're going to be very impressed, I should think.'

'I usually am,' I agreed. I'd grown lazy in my chair by the fire while he wrote, and felt much more inclined toward him than I had several hours ago.

We barely ever spoke of our problem: of our relationship and the innumerable consequences if we were ever discovered, but it weighed heavily on us both. My status as a widower would not protect us from suspicion forever, after all, but as Holmes began to read, I was surprised to learn I was a widower no longer – that I'd apparently married again, and gone away.

When he finished, he set the pages aside. 'I doubt we'll be able to keep up the fiction under scrutiny, though. You shall have to stop publishing, and I shall have to fade into obscurity.'

'It is a worthy sacrifice for me,' I said.

'For me as well,' he replied, leaning in, and then our rooms grew hushed for a while – with the occasional gasp – as we appreciated several of his solution's many benefits.

CHAPTER TWENTY

HE WAS SITTING BY THE FIRE WHEN I ARRIVED HOME FROM A NIGHT OUT at my club, his hands steepled before his mouth. His right shirtsleeve was still buttoned at his wrist; his left was rolled back to the elbow.

Neither of us said a word. I sat in the chair across from him and took him by the wrists, feeling absently for his pulse. It beat steadily underneath his skin.

'I haven't,' he said suddenly, giving voice to my thought. 'I wanted to. I even bought the bottles. But I knew – I didn't want to give you cause to leave.' He gestured over, and sure enough, I saw two glass bottles sitting on the table, gleaming innocently in the lamplight. They still looked full.

Carefully, not trusting myself yet to speak, I lifted his left hand to my mouth, kissing the pale underside of his wrist before rolling his cuff back down and buttoning it into place. 'I will never leave,' I promised solemnly. 'Whatever you do, I will never leave you, Sherlock.'

His lips parted on a shaky inhale. 'Get rid of them, John,' he pleaded. 'Please destroy them.'

I did so, and then I sat with him, holding both his hands in mine until the night was through and the dark sky finally began to turn to bronze.

Everything was still, but change was coming.

Sherlock's hand slid through the bedsheets, seeking out mine. Our fingers tangled together in the last shadows of the night, warm and soft; his palm pressed close against mine. 'I think we should leave Baker Street,' he whispered into the hush.

I inhaled slowly, exhaled slower. 'Where shall we go?' I whispered back.

There was a shift across the pillows as he looked at me; I looked back. His eyes were soft in the early light. 'You don't protest?'

'No. You've been taking fewer clients; I've been taking notes to write a book. I think perhaps it's time for us to move on from this life. I assume you know already.'

'Sussex, I should think.'

I laughed softly, wondering how long he had been planning our shared retirement. 'All right,' I agreed. 'Sussex.'

'So it's settled,' he said, raising our hands to examine them, illuminated by the creeping morning. 'It's time for the next adventure. You'll write your book, and I'll study apiculture, and we shall see what good we can do at loving one another.'

'It sounds perfect,' I said, drawing his hand down to kiss the back of it. 'It will be just us, then. Just you and me.'

'And the bees.'

I smiled and closed my eyes. 'Yes. And the bees.'

It was a strange thing, to say goodbye to London, to Baker Street.

Of course we would be back – Holmes would not be able to resist an evening in town for the symphony or an especially desperate plea for a private consultation from Scotland Yard, but I suspected we would have our hands quite full out in the countryside, and our best intentions of visiting were likely to be waylaid often.

Still, London was our city: where we had found each other, where we had followed each other. We had run down these alleys together, sat in these restaurants, listened to these gossips and these newsboys and these society ladies, going about their trades. It was a familiarity that I was increasingly nostalgic over as our days there came to a close.

'We'll see them again,' Holmes said to me, as I watched Lestrade and Gregson depart down Baker Street. Their good-byes had been brief and mannerly, no more than professional courtesy on the surface, but their handshakes had betrayed their true regrets at our leaving.

'It will be different, though,' I said.

Holmes stepped close behind me, wrapped an arm loosely around my waist: an easy, unexpected comfort. 'It will,' he said. 'But different isn't bad, John.'

'No,' I agreed, relaxing into him. 'I'm sure it'll be for the better.'

'You're different here,' Holmes said, our second week at the little cottage on the Downs. He was down to his shirtsleeves, smoking a pipe, smiling around the mouthpiece.

'Different how?' I asked, setting aside my pen. The stories now were no more than journal entries, but the habit was too well established to give it up entirely, even if they did go to a dispatch box rather than a publisher's press.

'I haven't quite sorted it out yet,' he answered. He rose from his chair quickly and came to bend around me at the desk. 'I think I know you too well to see the change as it's happening, the way a man can't see his own hair growing out until he's in need of the barber. Give me time, though. I'll get to the bottom of it.'

'I believe it,' I said, reaching up to him before he could spirit himself away. 'I know your methods.'

I already knew what he was seeing, though. I felt it every foggy morning, in every cup of tea or violin song drifting into the heathers. It was a warm, soaring feeling, the way a bird might feel in flight; I felt bigger, somehow, more open in my chest, as though for the first time in my life, I could take a full breath.

Epilogue

Sunlight creeps across the garden, bright and burnishing as it washes over the flowers. There's something poised about the world in the mornings, something simple and serene and suspended, as though a breath has been taken in, and is waiting to be released.

It is into this peace that Sherlock Holmes has walked with me.

The shadows of our life have begun to fade, and I am no longer surprised by the refuge we have found here, with our hands clasped together and our faces turned up to the sun. We have abandoned our hiding places, and it no longer surprises me to look up and find him looking back at me.

Not observing. Not deducing.

Just looking. Just knowing that we are together, and we are here.

There are still adventures. There are still papers towering with things we are not yet ready to forget; there are still books brimming with things we might yet want to know. There are still evenings spent poring over this problem or that, and musings that last long into the watches of the night.

But there are also kisses that no longer fade away with the darkness, and a promise that no longer goes unspoken after the shadows recede.

Every night comes to a close, and somewhere over the horizon, a new dawn breaks.

ACKNOWLEDGMENTS

Thanks to Leslie, for her work on this project as a beta, a cheerleader, and a shoulder to cry on over the last months of this project as well as the last few years of everything else, and to LeighAnne, for solving all my problems one panic at a time, and to the rest of the pocket gays for being pocket gays. No idea what anyone does without a set.

Thanks to Amy for her work as a beta, and especially for introducing me to John Yorke's guide to dramatic writing, *Into the Woods*, and for our endless discussions over story structure and analysis.

Thanks to Moony for her work as a beta as well, particularly with finding the Victorian voice through the haze of all my modernity and anachronisms.

Thanks to Erin, even though she'll never read this, for not even blinking at the things I get myself into. You're my person, friend.

Thanks to Wendy, for asking me to participate in this project. Publishing original work was always a 'someday, when I'm really ready' kind of dream – thank you for bringing someday up to now.

Finally, thanks to the Sherlock Holmes fandom for all the enthusiasm and acceptance I have found with you over the years, for listening to my stories and asking always for more, for your own creativity and dedication and thoughtfulness, and for all your stories which have inspired and improved my own. When I was alone in the darkness, you opened your arms and gave me back my words. There's nothing so beautiful as that.

ABOUT THE AUTHOR

Darcy Lindbergh has been a Holmes enthusiast for years, devouring and enjoying every adaptation she can get her hands on. Aside from writing original fiction and fanfiction, she enjoys cross-stitching fine art patterns, compiling extremely long to-do lists, and blogging about life, the universe, and Holmes and Watson on Tumblr (@watsonshoneybee) and Twitter (@darcylindbergh). She lives in the American Midwest with her dog, a beautiful good girl who is also called Darcy.

ABOUT THE BOOK

The sections of the story you have just read are precisely 221 words each, with the final word of every one beginning with B.

Inspired by 221B Baker Street, the address of the world's first consulting detective, this prose style is a unique way of telling tales about a detective and his doctor.

A QUESTION OF TIME by Jamie Ashbird

Sherlock Holmes whether he's a grimy student in 1980, a consulting detective in 47BCE, or a smitten neighbour in 1969, will always find his... John Watson whether he is a military doctor in 1917, an angry Saxon with an axe in 1086, or a priest in 1603. A Question of Time is an illustrated journey through the ages told by our heroes, by their friends, and by a scorched manuscript. Illustrated by Janet Anderton.

A STUDY IN VELVET AND LEATHER by K Caine

Sharing a flat with Sherlock Holmes should not have posed a problem for John Watson – after all, Watson is gay, Holmes is a woman, and the arrangement is financially convenient. But when Holmes takes on a complex case involving Irene Adler and a scandalous photograph, she turns to Watson for assistance. The case leads them everywhere from the opera to a secret Victorian BDSM club, and Watson soon finds himself questioning his partnership with Holmes, his sexuality, and his understanding of himself.

A DREAM TO BUILD A KISS ON by Narrelle M Harris

John Watson, invalided army doctor and sometime artist, and Sherlock Holmes, consulting detective, become flatmates and friends in contemporary London. Love grows too, despite past betrayals and present dangers – for where you have Holmes and Watson, there too are Moriarty and Moran. A Dream to Build a Kiss On explores love and family, trust and betrayal, brothers and brothers-in- arms, forgiveness and revenge, in an ongoing tale told 221 words at a time. Illustrated by Caroline Jennings.

www.ingramcontent.com/pod-product-compliance
Lightning Source LLC
Chambersburg PA
CBHW051927240626
47153CB00004B/1396